UNCHANGING
Whys

Michael,

I hope you enjoy this novel.

Merry christmas!

UNCHANGING *Whys*

T. L. Craig

ARCHWAY
PUBLISHING

Archway Publishing books may be ordered through booksellers or by contacting:

Archway Publishing
1663 Liberty Drive
Bloomington, IN 47403
www.archwaypublishing.com
1 (888) 242-5904

ISBN: 978-1-4808-1802-6 (sc)
ISBN: 978-1-4808-1801-9 (hc)
ISBN: 978-1-4808-1803-3 (e)

Library of Congress Control Number: 2015907108

Print information available on the last page.

Archway Publishing rev. date: 06/05/2015

Prologue

IT WAS THE SUMMER OF 1983 and I was 12 years old. The group '*New Edition*' just released their debut song, '*Candy Girl*'. My sisters and I knew that we would marry someone in the band. I remember that time well because that was also the year that my father passed from a stroke. I was too young to really know what was going on. Even as he lay in the hospital, my mom would take my sisters and me to visit. I would see him lying there hopeless.

My father and my mother never married. In fact, when my mother conceived my sisters and me, my father was married with another woman. My mother had six girls and never married. Issue number one "I was born into sin."

My name is China Barston. I was born in a town called New Berry, Illinois and I lived there my whole childhood. New Berry is a small town in a suburb outside of Chicago, Illinois. I attended grammar and high schools in that town. Growing up in New Berry was peaceful. There was never a want for anything. My mother, even though a single parent, raised my five siblings and I well. We wore the best of clothes and always had full meals, three times daily. From oldest to youngest: Alexa, Nubia, Donte, Amber, China and Tena; those are the names of all six of us. We were a close knit family. Even though we were close, there were age gaps, so our interests were different.

Due to the sheltered life that my mother raised us under, we were what some would say, "naïve".

Here is my story.

Chapter One

"CHINA, WHERE ARE YOU GOING stomping your feet, like you 'bout to march in an army?" her sister, Nubia asked.

"I have to get out of this house. We never have a chance to go out with our friends. Terry's parents let her stay out all the time and they don't say anything," whined China.

"Girl, you better stop trying to see through other people's mirrors. You don't know everything about everybody's home life. Just because Terry's able to go out all the time, doesn't mean that she's having more fun. Be cool," said Nubia.

"Well, one day I'm going to be able to do whatever I want, whenever I want, and no one's going to be able to stop me. Watch." China said with her arms folded.

"Good luck, duck butt." Nubia laughed as she walked away.

China and her sisters spent a lot of time on the stoop in the front of their house. Often times, they were only allowed to look out the window. Their mother's younger brother died after a bar fight when he was twenty-one. Their mother was protective of them because she was still holding on to the guilt of not being able to protect her brother.

One summer day, China was sitting on the front porch, and saw a lady standing on the corner. Men would pull up in nice cars and the lady would get in. It seemed like it happened every hour. China thought, *Wow, that lady sure has a lot of boyfriends.*

The lady looked to be in her mid to late twenties. She always dressed in these short prissy dresses and wore high heels. The lady lived in the apartment building across the street.

The block China lived on was a neighborhood street. Kids would play all day long in the summer, and no one would bother them. Also in the apartment building across the street were a diner, a doctor's office, and a pharmacy. Inside the doctor's office was a candy store. China and her sisters nick named the candy store, "*the doctor's store.*" China and her sisters would go to the doctor's store daily. Their mother would give them a dollar a week for allowance, and they would spend it all at the doctor's store.

One day, China went across the street to the doctor's store. The lady who had all the boyfriends came in as China was leaving. When China saw her face up close, she noticed it was wrinkled. Her makeup was running, and she had this huge hole in her panty hose. She heard the clerk at the pharmacy call the lady Maura. The clerk handed Maura a bag of pills, and she left. China always wondered why Maura had so many boyfriends, and why she looked so sad up close.

China had one friend, Terry. They would do everything together, well everything they could when China was allowed. Terry came to ask China if she could go to the baseball game at the park on the next block.

"Girl, I don't know. My mother wants me to be where she can see me," China replied.

"I almost forgot that you were on house arrest until you turn eighteen." They both laughed.

"Well, you know that Crawl is going to be there," Terry added.

"Crawl? Are you sure?" China asked excitedly.

"Yep, I saw him yesterday at the movies and he was like, 'Terry, you should bring China to Becks Park to the baseball game tomorrow.' I told him I would try," Terry said.

"Cross your fingers, girl. Let me ask my mother," China said, and Terry crossed two fingers on both hands and smiled.

China was hoping her mother would let her go just this once. But in her mind, she knew that her mother was going to say no. Her mother knew that thugs and misguided kids hung out at those games. But, she had to ask. Her future baby daddy, Crawl was going to be there. Her mother was in the basement ironing.

"Ma, can I please go to Becks to watch the game?" she begged her mother.

"Ask Nubia or Alexa if they'll go with you," her mom replied. She didn't look up and continued to iron clothes.

"Why, Ma? Terry is going to be there. It's only right around the corner," China whined.

Her mother stopped ironing. She sat the iron on the ironing board, looked up, put her hand on her hip, looked at China, and said, "ask me again, and the answer will be no. Ask your sisters," she ordered.

China knew that her sisters were not going to watch a baseball game. They had 'more important things to do.'

"Nubia, can you go to Becks with me to watch the game?" China asked.

Nubia said, "Not."

Alexa was nowhere to be found. China just had to get to that game to see Crawl. She went to the basement and told her mother that Alexa was going to go with her. Her mother told her she could go.

"What? Your mom let you out the castle?" Terry asked jokingly.

"Girl, shut up. Let's go before she changes her mind," China said, and they ran down the front steps.

The girls arrived at the park and sure enough, Crawl and his gang were there sitting in the stands watching the game. China and Terry sat directly in front of the guys.

Ray Ray, Crawl's best friend, asked Terry jokingly, "So, who's the new girl?"

China turned around and smiled at Crawl. She then rolled her eyes at Ray Ray and told him to shut up.

"Ease up off my girl, man," said Crawl, elbowing Ray Ray. Crawl scooted between China and Terry. He leaned on China and said, "I'm glad you're here."

"Me too," China replied, grinning.

After the game, Crawl walked China and Terry to the corner. "So, China, are we going to do this or what?" Crawl asked.

"Do what?" China replied, smiling, and gazing into Crawls eyes.

"Do us," Crawl said, and returned her gaze.

China looked away and said, "Yep."

"Don't play with me, girl," Crawl said, and he grabbed her hands.

"I don't play," China pulled him close and she kissed him on the cheek. She backed away wondering how she could do that.

Crawl seemed presently surprised and said, "Tell yo' girl I got you then."

"Terry, I'm good," China said.

"Are you sure, girl?" Terry asked.

"Yep, my boo got me," China replied and Terry proceeded home without her.

"So, do you want to go to my house?" Crawl asked.

"Is your mother home?"

"Nope, she at work."

"I don't know if that's a good idea." China said and pulled away.

"Well, either you down or you ain't. I got all these chicks trying to get with me, and I'm spending so much time trying to get with the wind. Tell me something." Crawl backed away further.

"Okay, I'll go. I have to be home by six or my mom will call the police."

"I got-chu." Crawl said, smiled and took China by the hand.

Crawl lived two blocks from Becks Parks, three blocks from China's house. He was an only child and his mother was an ambulance technician. She worked all the time. His father was an alcoholic who sat on the corner all day long.

They arrived at Crawl's house and sat on the couch.

"So, what are we going to do?" China asked.

"What?" Crawl asked.

"I think we need to slow it down," said China and she moved toward the other end of the couch.

"Slow what down? This? Why?" He moved closer to her and started to kiss her neck.

"I don't know. I just want to talk. Let's watch TV or something."

"Girl, you don't think *we* here to watch TV, do you? Maybe I should just not be into you and focus on some of the other girls who are ready for this."

"What do you mean?"

"Don't worry about it." Crawl smirked and opened the door for China to leave.

China grabbed her jacket and left. On her way home, she felt very sad. She just knew that Crawl was the one for her. She got to the corner near the doctor's store where she saw Maura and a guy. It looked like they were arguing. The guy began to hit Maura's face. Maura was screaming and crying. No one would help her. The guy yelled at her and told her to get in there and clean up, pointing toward the building they lived in. Maura stumbled up the stairs. The guy rubbed his nose, and looked up. China noticed that the man saw her watching. She stood there not moving one inch. The man rolled his eyes at her and walked up the stairs behind

Maura. China was in shock. She had never seen anything so violent before. After the door closed behind him, China ran home.

When China got home, her mother was sitting in the living room waiting with a belt. She knew someone was in trouble. "What's wrong Ma?" China asked.

"Child, where you been?"

"I was at Becks at the game." China replied nervously.

"Who went with you?"

"Terry, and I asked Alexa."

"Did Alexa go with you?" Her mother tapped her foot angrily and waited for a response.

"No, ma'am."

"Didn't I tell you to go with her or Nubia?" her mother yelled.

"Yeah, ma, but they wouldn't go." China began to cry.

Her mom whipped her good. "Don't you ever discard my orders again, you hear me?" her mother cried, and tears ran down her face.

"Yeah, Mom, Ow!! I'm sorry," China cried.

"Now, get up there, and get to bed without dinner. Don't you ask to leave this house until you turn fifty-two, you hear?" she yelled.

Ms. Barston was crying more than China.

China sat in that tub sore and bruised. When she got to bed, Tena, her youngest sister brought her a sandwich. "Girl, what made you lie to momma like that?" she whispered.

"Shut up," China replied, and she knocked the sandwich from her little sister's hand.

"That's what you get dummy," Tena said quietly and laid in the bottom bunk bed.

That summer was the longest summer China had ever experienced. Not only did her mother not allow her to leave the house without one of her older sisters, China learned that Terry and her family moved out of state to Georgia because her father had gotten another position at his corporation. It was the most boring summer for China. She began to write notes to herself about how things would be if she had more freedom. She imagined being outside all night playing with Terry. She imagined going where ever she wanted, whenever she wanted. It made her very happy inside. She wrote down places she would go like the mall, the movies, and baseball games every day.

The summer had ended, and it was time for China to begin the 8th grade. She thought, *I will almost be an adult and my freedom would be near.*

China got pretty decent grades in school. Her favorite subject was math. She knew one day that she would be rich and that she would need to keep track of her money. She did not attend many after school functions or events. Since Terry's relocation, she spent most days alone. That was until she met her new best friend, Macon.

Chapter Two

ONE DAY, CHINA WALKED TO her locker and noticed a girl that she had never seen before. The girl was wearing really expensive jeans, and a leather jacket. She looked at China and asked, "Excuse me, can you please tell me where I can find the Office Education Lab?"

China relied, "Sure. It's room 318. Just turn right and it's at the end of this hall," she pointed down the corridor.

"Thank you. Oh, my name is Macon, by the way," she extended her hand.

"Hi Macon. I'm China. Are you new here?" China shook Macon's hand.

"Yes."

"Welcome to New Berry Jr. High," China smiled.

China and Macon became very good friends. They had a lot in common. They were even in some of the same classes.

It was spirit week in their 8th grade, and Friday. Students were to dress in pajamas. China and Macon decided to wear the same type of pajamas, but different colors.

The girls were eating lunch. Crawl walked to their table and jokingly began to talk to them, "well, wehell, what do we have here? Twins?"

China pretended not to see him. She was still angry at his behavior last summer.

Macon knew about what happened. Sticking up for her friend, she rolled her eyes, and replied to Crawl's remarks. "At least we don't look like yo' ugly tail."

"Ugly? Ugly? Gal, who you calling ugly?" he asked.

"You the only other person over here."

"You wish you could get with this," he said and pointed to himself.

"Whatever boy. Bye," Macon said. She rolled eyes again, and put her hands in his face.

"Yeah. Okay," Crawl replied. The lunch room supervisor began to walk near the table, and Crawl walked away.

"Girl, what did you ever see in that boogaloo?" Macon asked. They both giggled and walked to their classes.

On the walk home that day, China and Macon approached Macon's block. "See you for the game tomorrow Macon," China said.

Macon turned the corner to proceed to home. "Okay China. Bye."

China was two blocks from her house, she noticed Crawl creeping around the corner. She thought, *I hope this dummy do not say anything to me.* Crawl looked at her as he got closer. She thought about turning the block before hers in hopes to avoid him. She changed her mind and thought, *I'm not thinking about him, keep walking, don't make eye contact, be cool.* Crawl bounced his head up and down.

"You still running from this, girlee?" he asked.

"Boy, aint nobody running from you. You ain't nothing to run from."

"Now, you know you still want this," he giggled.

"Whatever."

"All you have to do is say the word. You know you have my heart," he said and put his hands on his chest.

All China could do is recall how much of an idiot Crawl was to her.

"You know something, if you weren't such an idiot that day after that game last summer, we probably would be a couple right now. You really surprised me. Bye Crawl," she said and she started to walk away.

Crawl grabbed her hand and kissed the inside of her hand softly. "I am so sorry. I can't get you out of my mind. All I think about is you. Can I have another chance? Please?" he begged.

China saw the look on his face and could not believe that she still had a liking feeling toward him.

She snatched her hand and said firmly, "I said bye Crawl." She walked home, quickly.

The next morning, China woke up to complete her chores to avoid punishment. Her mother began to allow China and her sisters' privileges to attend school games. Her mother told her that she felt the school events were safe.

"What time is the game over China?" her mother asked.

"6:30, no later than 7."

"You and Macon come straight home, you hear?" her mother demanded.

"Yes, ma'am," China replied, and she left to pick up Macon for the game.

Macon's parents were well off. They both worked for the V. A. Hospital. Her parents bought her all the best, brand named clothes. She was always allowing China to borrow her clothes. China's mother always bought her and her sisters' good quality clothes. She would never buy them brand named anything.

"Hey, Macon. You ready to go, girl?" China asked, and walked in Macon's door way.

"Yep. Let me grab my wallet and jacket," Macon replied, and ran to grab her belongings.

They walked to the school. When they arrived, Crawl and his gang were there. Crawl looked China directly into her eyes. China walked past him and rolled her eyes at him.

Two girls approached Macon and China out of not where and began to put their hands in their faces. They accused them of trying to get with their *'dudes'*. China was quite surprised. She was in no way after Crawl or anybody else for that matter.

"What are you talking about!" yelled China.

"I see you stalking my man!" the rugged, street girl yelled back.

"And who's your man?"

"You know dag-on-well that Crawl is my man. Why are you trying to get with my man? I'll wipe you all over this gym," the street girl threatened, bumping up against China.

"I have no interest in Crawl at all. He's always running up behind me. You better get out of my face!" China screamed and backed up away.

The school guard separated the girls from each other. They warned the girls to keep it down or they would be asked to leave and possibly be placed in detention if they fight.

Back in the '80s there were seldom any school suspensions. The school officials believed in counseling the students to get them on track. They believed that keeping a child in school, would be more beneficial to the child than kicking them out of school.

"Watch yo' back," the street girl snarled. Both girls walked to their seats to watch the game.

China could hardly focus on the game with the street girl watching her the whole game. She thought, *why on earth could this girl think that she was interested in Crawl.* She refused to walk home that evening. She had never had a fight and wasn't about to ruin her *'good girl'* image fighting over something that was not true.

China called Alexa. Alexa drove her and Macon home from the

game. When she got in the house, she called Macon to discuss what happened.

"China, what was that all about?" ask Macon.

"Girl, I have no idea. That girl's out of her mind. I have no idea who she is, or where she came from."

"Well, she's in my science class. Her name is Sheila, and she's way out there. Why would she think you are after Crawl like that?"

"Didn't you just hear me say that she needs some type of medication? She's completely crazy. I hope I don't ever see that psycho again. I am not going to worry about it. If she come at me again, I'll just bust her jaw. That's all," China laughed.

"Now girl, you know you can't fight." Macon replied and they both laughed. They said their good nights.

China couldn't sleep at all that night. She was worried that Sheila would try to find her and gang up on her with her crew. She decided that she'd try to call Crawl after church the next day to find out what was going on. She thought, if anyone could clear this mess up, it would have to be Crawl.

Church service ended. When China arrived home, she called Crawl. His mother answered the phone as usual.

"Good afternoon Mrs. Rogers, may I speak with Crawl?" she asked respectfully.

"He ain't home. Bye." Mrs. Rogers hung up the phone.

China began to wonder where Crawl could be. She looked outside did not see anyone. She felt nervous in her stomach. She contemplated on whether or not to tell her older sisters so that they could help her with the situation. She decided not to tell anyone in her family. China thought her sisters would tell their mother and their mother would not allow China to leave the house again. She decided to handle the situation on her own. That evening, she tried to call Crawl again.

"Good evening Mrs. Rogers. May I speak with Crawl?" China asked. Crawl's mother called for him to come to the phone.

"Who-dis?" he said.

"Crawl, this is China."

"Wehell, it's about time you came to your senses. You may as well come on over here right now so we can handle our business."

"Boy, this ain't no social call. What the heck is Sheila?"

"Are you jealous? Girl, you ain't got to be all jealous. I told you, you got me. Just say the word."

"Boy, are you crazy? I'm not thinking about you. This thing is coming at me like I'm a chicken bone and she trying to eat. You better tell her what's what. You better straighten her out."

"I ain't got nothing to do with that. That's between you and her. You scared?" he teased.

"Boy, if you don't end this mess, I will never, ever talk to you again. You hear me?" she warned.

"Okay. Calm down honey. I got you. So, are you coming over today or not?"

China hung up the phone extremely upset. She couldn't believe how Crawl thought this was some type of game.

China was a little nervous when she went to school that Monday. Whatever Crawl said to Sheila must have worked. She saw Sheila at lunch. Sheila looked at her, rolled her eyes, and said nothing.

The eighth grade school year ended. China graduated junior high school. She attended New Berry High School. Her mother began to allow the girls even more freedom.

Chapter Three

CHINA EXPERIENCED ONE OF HER best years in high school during her Sophomore Year. She began to get more involved with school programs. She and Macon's friendship grew closer.

China's drama teacher persuaded her into participating in the Miss New Berry High School Pageant. Before then, China had never danced in school, or at parties. She was a little nervous, but she agreed.

Ms. Oliver, China's drama teacher assigned another teacher to assist China with preparing for the dance. They selected a song from the TV show '*Fame*' entitled '*Star Maker*.'

China practiced after school and at home. Nubia helped her practice for the dance a great deal. Macon also provided advice.

"China girl, loosen up," Nubia said, "why you acting so stiff?"

"Girl, this is hard," she replied, trying to keep her balance, twirling around. "I never saw you trying to do anything like this. I would like a little more leniency."

"Girl, if you want something, you have to work hard at it," Nubia said, trying to imitate Debbie Allen from the show, '*Fame*'. She held a stick she picked up from the back yard. They all laughed.

"So, who are you going to ask to escort you in the pageant?" Macon asked.

"I don't know. The guys at our school are so blah." China replied, and looked at her stance in the mirror.

"Girl, they not marrying you that night. They just need to look right in a suit, and walk you to the stage. I saw the dress momma asked Mrs. Diamond to make you. It's so beautiful," Nubia added.

"I don't have a lot of time to decide. I'm probably going to ask somebody that don't even go to our school," she smirked.

That night China was up all night thinking about who she could ask to escort her in the pageant. She never had a boyfriend. The only boy she even liked since her birth was Crawl. She thought, *now why did I have to think about him before I fell asleep. He gone make me have a nightmare.* She laughed and the thought made her smile.

The next day at school, China and Macon were at lunch eating. Crawl approached the girls at their table. "Uh-Hum, so what color are we wearing to the pageant, Mrs. New Berry High?" He asked China.

"Macon, do you hear somebody?" she asked. She turned her head from side to side and pretended not to see Crawl standing in front of them.

"Naw. I thought I heard a fly, but, nobody important," Macon replied. She and China high-fived each other as if they won a prize. They continued to look at each other, as if Crawl was not in their presence.

"Come on lil' momma. You know we'll make the school spin when we walk down that gym floor together. My momma already taking my suit to the cleaners. I just need you to tell me what color shirt and tie."

"Now what make you think that I would ask you of all people to take me to the pageant?" China continued, "I ain't even trying to have Mrs. Boogaloo come at me again," still thinking about Sheila.

"If you talking about Shelia, we never were. You know you the only one for me. I keep tellin you that lil momma. Plus, she don't even go to this school no more. Okay, you better ask me before one of those other girls grab me up. You know I'm all of that." Crawl picked up China's hand and kissed it gently.

China was getting butterflies in her stomach. Macon, snatched China's hand from Crawl's and told her to snap out of it. Crawl left the table.

China was in awe. She could not believe that she still had feelings for him.

"Tell me you are not feeling this rug rat, and please tell me you are not even thinking about asking him to the pageant. Please." Macon begged.

"What other options do I have?" China asked and she pointed to Early Mornings. The rumor around the school was that his mother name him Early because his last name was Mornings. China always thought he looked just like morning too, with jerry curl juice all over his forehead and neck. They both laughed.

That day, after pageant practice, Crawl was standing in the school hallway waiting for China. "Lil Momma, what time does your watch say. Tick-tock," He said, looking down at his wrist watch.

"Okay. You can escort me in the pageant. But, no touching my anything, and no talking, and no breathing. You hear?"

Crawl replied with a nodding up and down of his head. To obey her wishes, he took his paper tablet from his back pack to write, "What color shirt and tie?" He ended with a smiley face.

"We're wearing lilac."

He wrote a big heart and in the middle wrote, "You got it," he smiled, danced, and walked away.

China thought that she could not believe that she just asked this coo coo to take her to the pageant. Oh well, she thought, *one less THING to worry about.*

It was the night of the pageant. Crawl's mom and China's mom had been in contact with each other to plan the evening. Crawl's mom offered to drive them. China told her mom no and that they would meet at the school.

Nubia persuaded China to ride to the pageant with Crawl. She assured her that she would ride with them. China agreed.

China performed her dance. It was now time for the contestants to walk into the gym in formal wear. China and Crawl walked side by side. At first, China would not let Crawl touch her hands. Nubia took China's hand and gave it to Crawl. Crawl grinned to the walls.

"Okay, but, don't touch nothing else on me," she told him.

They walked to their places on the gym floor. When they reached their marks, Crawl pulled a single rose out of his suit jacket pocket and gave it to China. He then kissed her lightly on the cheeks. She could not do anything but smile. The audience clapped in awe.

China did not win the pageant contest. But, she felt at that moment that she did win a friend, if nothing else in Crawl. She saw a completely different side of him.

After the pageant was over, Crawl walked over to China and asked her if she wanted to go with him to the after party at the city's recreation hall. Without hesitation, she said told him she would go. They had fun at the party. They laughed and danced.

"Crawl, I'm going to get ready to leave. I have things to do in the morning," China said.

"What, are you eight-nine years old? Live a little, will ya?"

"Here we go again. Bye." China replied and she turned to walk out.

"Hold up lil momma. I'm just playing with you. I'm not going to let you leave by yourself. What do you think I am? I will get you home." Crawl signaled for his friend that had a car. His friend went to tell his girlfriend something. He and Crawl left to take China home.

"China, this is Mark. Mark, this is China." Crawl introduced them.

"You go to New Berry High, Mark? I haven't seen you around," she asked.

"Nope, I don't go to school no more."

"Must be nice. What is it that you do?"

"You ask a lot of questions for somebody who can't even drive yet," he replied, defensively.

"I just like to know who I talk to or who I get a ride from. That's all."

"China, he good people. Would you just take a chill pill? Man come on. Let's get this one home before we have to take lie detector tests," Crawl interrupted and giggled.

"I got-chu," Mark replied.

Crawl got in the back seat with China. He began to play with her necklace.

"That was a great dance," Crawl whispered in China's ear.

"Thanks," she replied, softly.

"When you gone dance like that for me?" he asked softly and nibbled her ear.

China felt tingly, but she liked it and didn't make him stop. "I don't dance for just anybody."

"You know I'm somebody. You know we been feeling each other for a long time. Let's do this thing, alright?" He gently moved her chin toward his face and kissed her on the lips. She did not stop him. They kissed for a long time. They pulled up in front of her house. He walked her to the front door.

"I'll call you later. Good night." He watched her walk into the house.

"Good night." She closed the door gently.

That night was a good night for China. She thought about Crawl and the kiss all night.

The next morning, China got up to complete her chores so that she could go to Macon's to tell her everything that happened. When she got to Macon's house, Macon was waiting. "Hey girl. How was your evening?" She did not spare time.

"It was wonderful. I think I'm falling for Crawl. He was so gentle."

"Well, if that's what you like. I mean, I think you can do a lot better. Even Early Mornings is a better look for you than Crawl."

"I think I'm going to play this thing out to see where it goes. Who knows? Maybe, he will be my baby daddy after all one day." They laughed.

"So, what happened? Tell me everything."

"We went to the after party at the Rec. We talked, laughed and danced all night. On the way home we kissed the entire time. I'm really feeling him." China smiled in a daze.

"Well, sounds like this may be something. Have you spoken to him since last night?"

"Nope. But, he did tell me that he'd call me."

"Good luck. I hope yawl live happily ever after then."

China did not hear from Crawl all day Saturday, or all day Sunday. She assured herself that he definitely wouldn't get another chance.

Monday morning at school, China saw Crawl at his locker. She walked past him and he began to talk as if he didn't do anything.

"Hey, lil momma. Come here."

China walked over to him to see what he had to say. "How was your weekend?" he continued.

"What do you mean? How was my weekend? You didn't bother to call me after we shared the longest kiss. What are you taking me for?"

"I did try to call you Saturday morning. Donte answered the phone. She didn't tell you I called? I was waiting all weekend for you to call me back."

"She didn't tell me you called," China replied unapologetically.

"So are we good then?"

"I have to think about it."

"It's a good thing you in that drama class. You're going to be on the big screens one day."

"Whatever." China said and she walked away.

She left Crawl standing in the halls. They did not hook back up that year. China could not trust him with her heart.

Chapter Four

THE NEXT FEW YEARS PASSED, China and her sisters moved on in their lives.

Alexa was in nursing at a local hospital. She had her own apartment.

Nubia lived with her husband in the next town.

Amber went to junior college. However, she never completed a course. She went to junior college four years and had a job at the diner.

Donte was in college in Maryland.

China is finishing her senior year in high school.

Tena is finishing her sophomore year in high school.

Their mother was in a relationship with Willie Greene. He owned a construction business.

"China, go to the diner across the street and tell Mr. Simms to let you buy a carton of eggs." her mother ordered. She gave China a five dollar bill.

China purchased the eggs. She was walking out of the diner. The guy that beat Maura up five years ago blocked the door with his foot to prevent China from exiting.

"Excuse you," China told him rolling her eyes in anger.

"Well, pardon me miss," the guy said. He backed away and took his cap off his head. He took his foot off the door and opened it for China. She walked out.

China was walking out the door, she looked up and bumped into a guy. He turned around and it was Crawl, her old baby daddy.

"Boy, where you been?" she asked, "and why don't you come to school anymore?"

"Hey, boo. I been around. I got better things to do." He replied, looking down in embarrassment.

"Better than school? Well, anyway, bye."

"Wait, hold up lil' momma. Why you always runnin' away?"

"I want to get out your way. You probably got some other chicks waiting and I'm drama free."

"You know you the only one for me. What you got in the bag?" He said. He began to tug the brown paper bag playfully.

"Eggs for my mom."

"Uh-oh, are you inviting me for breakfast?"

"Boy, please. My momma not gone let anybody that don't have time for school, eat her eggs," she replied. She took his hand off the bag with her index finger and thumb.

"Right, right. So you ready to get with a dude or what?"

"If you going to get with this, you better come better than that."

"Okay. Seriously, can we hang out at my house and watch TV this weekend?" Crawl begged.

"Oh, now you wanna watch TV? I have to think about it."

"Okay. Don't wait too long," said Crawl. He opened the door for her to exit.

China got home. All she could think about was Crawl. She looked across the street at the diner. She saw him talking to that guy that beat up Maura. She knew in her mind that Crawl was up to no good. But, she was still feeling him. She called him on his house phone and his mother answered the phone. "Hello."

"Hello Mrs. Rogers, may I speak with Crawl."

"Girl, Crawl ain't here."

"Can you please tell him that China called?"

"Um hm, bye." His mother replied and hang up the phone.

China and Macon's friendship grew closer. They were true best friends. They did everything together.

She called Macon to tell her the events from the diner.

"Girl, tell me that you still not having fantasies over cool-mo-dee. Please tell me." Macon begged.

"It's just something about him. He has changed over the years and the roughness is starting to catch my eye."

"Girl, I am going to ask your mother to get you some bifocals, 'cuz you clearly have a vision problem. Girl, stay away from that rat. He's bad news. Promise me." Macon continued to plead to China.

"I will," she replied. "I have to go finish the laundry. I'll call you later. Bye."

"Okay, bye." Macon replied, as they hung up their phones.

Three days later China's doorbell rang. It was Crawl.

"China, some boy down here for you," Tena yelled for China to come downstairs to the door.

"Hey Crawl. Did your mom tell you I called?" China asked him.

"Hu? Yeah. Why do you think I'm here?" Crawl replied as if he was surprised that China called his house.

"Nice of you to return my call from three days ago."

"I been doing things, you know. Well, are we going to hang, or what?"

"We can hang here for a minute."

"Naw. Let's go to my friends spot. It's cool there."

"Where is it?"

"Across the street," Crawl responded. He pointed to the apartment building on the corner of China's house.

"You not talking about that guy I saw you talking to the other day?" China asked folding her arms.

"What guy?"

"The loser guy from the diner that always sits in there."

"Oh, that's my boy Dirty. He ain't nobody."

"Um, well he's not good people."

"Girl, dag, you always trying to be my momma."

"Call it whatever."

"What are you going to do?" Crawl asked, as he began to pull her closer. China started to reminisce about the kiss they shared.

"Okay, let me tell my mom." She replied. Just as she tried to turn, Crawl stopped her.

"Look, if you still gotta get permission, you may not be ready for this thing."

"Okay, okay, hold up a minute," she grabbed her jacket off the coat rack.

They walked across the street and entered into the apartment that Maura lived in. Maura was there with her head hung over looking at the floor.

Dirty sat next to Maura, and he was looking China up and down.

"'Sup yawl?" asked Crawl, when he and China walked in.

"Nothin' dude. Who is the little lady?" Dirty asked.

"This my, boo, lil' momma," Crawl replied, introducing China.

"Lil' momma," Dirty said. He gazed at China with his beady eyes, "do you remember me?"

China did not reply. She could not stop staring at Maura. She was thinking how sad and tired Maura looked.

"Man can she talk. Is she death or something?" Dirty asked Crawl. He started to show aggravation that China was not paying him any attention.

"Dirty, she's just shy that's all," Crawl replied.

"We ain't no shy bee's up in here," said Dirty. "We all like family."

"Crawl, I think I'm just going to talk to you some other time." China said sadly, and began to walk to the door.

"Hold on lil' momma. I'm just playing with ya. You ain't got to run all scared," Dirty said.

"Oh, ain't nobody scared of you. I just don't choose to hang around nobodies." China replied, with attitude. She rolled her eyes directly at Dirty.

"So, you miss bad lil' momma. We'll see how bad you is when I come over there and smack you," Dirty said. He raised from the couch and began to get up. He walked toward China.

Out of nowhere, Maura pulled herself up from the couch. She grabbed a beer bottle off the table and broke it across Dirty's head. He was knocked out cold.

"Dag Maura, what did you do?" Crawl asked in a state of shock.

"I, I, don't know," she replied, stuttering and shaking. "I just lost it for a minute. Is he dead?"

"I don't know," Crawl said. He walked over to Dirty to check for a pulse. "I don't feel a pulse. Man we better get out of here. I got too much on my back already."

"I can't leave here," she replied. "I don't have nowhere else to go. We need to get him out of here."

"I don't want any part of this," China cried. She sat in the corner, and watched. "Why can't we just call the ambulance and get him a doctor?"

"Girl, we all in this together," Maura said. "Don't you try and pretend you ain't all in this. This all yo fault anyway for trying to play lil' miss bad mamma jamma. Let's come back here tonight and get him out of here.

Crawl I need you to get one of those big black bags. Lil' Momma, be back here at 11 pm sharp."

"This is not my fault," China cried more. "I didn't tell you to hit him. I had nothing to do with this."

"If you don't come back here like I told you, I will make sure that this will be yo' fault, you hear?" Maura pointed her finger in China's face in a threatening manner.

"Crawl say something," China pleaded. "Tell, this lady I'm not in this, please?"

"China, come back at eleven. This will all be taken care of. I promise."

China ran home. She could not believe what just happened. She began to ponder, *do I tell momma? Do I call the police myself? I can't go back there. I can't.* All she could hear is Maura's voice tell her, '*be back here at eleven sharp.'*

China wanted to talk to Crawl to tell him that she was not going back to Maura's. She tried to call his house, but his mother answered the phone and told her that Crawl didn't live there anymore. Now China began to feel very scared. She thought, *What has she gotten herself into now? Who was Crawl? What other things did he have on his back?*

That night at 10:45 pm, China walked past her mother's room to see if she was sleep. Ms. Barston was sound asleep. China walked out the back door and headed across the street. Before she could reach the front yard, she saw sirens everywhere. She turned around and ran back into her house. She looked out the window. She saw the ambulance technician carrying a body bag. Maura was handcuffed and being placed in the police car. China did not know what was going on.

Maura raised her head. China watch her. They looked at each other directly into the eyes.

The next morning China tried to call Crawl's house again. His mother answered the phone crying. She said that Crawl had been killed at a girlfriend's house the night before. She said the police had the person that killed him.

The next year was a lot for China. Macon, her best friend of five years moved to France for a student exchange program. China graduated high school and was ready to begin her adult life.

Chapter Five

"GO COMMODORES, GO! DEFENSE! DEFENSE!" China and her boyfriend screamed enthusiastically as their university's basketball team played the final quarter in the playoff game.

China met Cory in the library at Vanderbilt University. Both attended college there. China was in her second year, studying business management. Cory was a pre-med student in graduate school. They immediately connected and had been boyfriend and girlfriend since they met.

The final buzzer sounded. "Yes, we won. We're number one!" China shouted as the whole school jumped in excitement to finally win their basketball championship after 8 years.

"Let's celebrate." Cory suggested as he kissed China softly on the lips.

"Let's." she replied.

There were several parties planned after the game. They decided to attend the party at the local disco club.

"Let's swing by my dorm room so that I can change," she suggested.

"Girl, you always have to change for every place we go. There's nothing wrong with what you have on. Don't you want to keep the school spirit?" Cory asked, hoping she would agree.

"Well, excuse me if I'm so fresh and so clean," she laughed.

"That, you are," he replied, helplessly.

They reached China's dorm room. She heard the phone ringing as she put her key in the door.

"Hello," China answered, breathing heavily, trying to catch her breath from rushing to answer the call.

"Hey China. How are you doing?" her mom asked.

"Hey Ma. I am so fine. We just won our championship game. How are you doing ma?"

"I'm well. Did you receive the package I mailed you last week?"

"Yes ma'am. I got it today. I was going to call you in the morning to let you know. Mom thank you so much. I know that times are hard. You don't have to send me so much."

"It's fine. I had a little extra. I just want to make sure that you have enough to get through," her mother replied, coughing.

"Yes ma'am. I really appreciate it. Hey mom, can you talk to Cory a few minutes while I get dressed?"

"Yes. Put my future son in law on the phone."

China handed Cory the phone, "good evening Mrs. Barston. How are you doing Ma'am?" Cory asked, respectfully.

"Hey my future son in law. I'm fine. How are you doing?" she asked boldly.

"I'm well ma'am," he replied, giggling.

"So, yawl about to go out? Where are yawl going?"

"Oh, we're going to this local lounge, where a lot of the other Commodores are going to celebrate the winning game. How is the weather there?"

"Cold. I promise I want to pack up and move there with yawl summer-time weather," they both laughed.

"Listen, SON, I won't keep yawl. Have fun. Tell your future wife to call me when she wake up in the morning."

China and Cory celebrated their team's victory and returned to their respective door rooms for the night.

Chapter Six

"GOOD MORNING MR. JACKSON. I still can't believe that our honeymoon is almost over." China told Cory and she kissed him on the lips. "I wish we could stay on this island for one more week."

"Me too," he replied. "But, you know I have to get back to the hospital to save lives."

I know, right? I am very much excited about my new position with Buckner Real Estate."

China and Cory married three years after China graduated college and Cory completed graduate school. She was offered a position as senior broker at the real estate company she has been working as a sales agent for the past year. She received her bachelor's degree in accounting. However, she decided at the end of her final the semester to pursue real estate.

Cory completed his residency at the Vanderbilt University Hospital in Nashville, Tennessee and is now a physician at the same hospital.

They live in Caryville, Tennessee, near the town they graduated college.

China's mother still lives in Illinois. She is aging and calls China every day for a daily report.

"Good afternoon ma," China said answering the phone. It was 3:45pm sharp, the time her mother called every day. If she did not answer the phone, her mother would leave a voicemail. China knew that it would be difficult to call her mother back because her mother would be on the phone trying to call her five siblings for their day reports. Willie, her mother's boyfriend was killed in an apparent robbery two years ago.

"Hey China. What are you doing?"

"I'm about to leave my office to head home," she continued, "I have a dinner meeting with a new client this evening."

"Sounds nice. Where are yawl going?"

"We are going to The Brown-N-Serve Steak House."

"Oh, I like that place. I can't wait to come visit so my new son-in-law could take me there again."

"Any time, mom. Just let me know when so I could get your ticket. How are you feeling today ma?"

"I'm fine. I went to the doctor and they gave me more medicine for the pain in my leg. I think I need that son-in-law of mine to come take a look."

"Has Donte been by to check on you today?"

"Yeah. But, you know she busy running behind that husband of hers and those four kids." She replied, coughing.

"Well, what about Amber, she lives in your house. When is the last time you saw her?" China asked. She began to feel angry at her sisters.

"Well, she was here this morning, and I ain't seen her since."

"Momma, how would you like to come stay here for a few months. We have this huge place and extra space just for you."

"Now you know I ain't trying to be 'round no newlyweds," her mother laughed. "I'm fine baby. Come see me soon."

"I will ma. I promise. I love you."

"I love you too baby. Bye."

"By ma." China said as they hung up their phones.

China began to worry about the tone in her mother's voice. She paged Donte's beeper and waited for a return call.

"Hey Donte." China said as she answered the phone.

"Hey China."

"How are you?"

"I'm doing me." Donte answered back, smugly.

"Well, when is the last time you went by to check on Momma?"

"I was there yesterday. She isn't only my responsibility, you know. I got all these kids," she replied with attitude in her voice.

"Okay girl. How are my niece and nephews?" China asked to change the subject.

"Girl, they are bad. They are driving me crazy. Hey, I think I'm going to send them to you."

"Go right ahead. I have to run. I'll talk to you later. Love you."

"Love you too. Bye." Donte replied. They hung up their phones.

China dreaded calling Amber. She was an older sister and had a huge drug addiction problem. She didn't know if she was coming or going sometimes. China prayed, *Lord, give me strength.* She paged Amber's beeper. Amber finally called back forty-five minutes later.

"Hey Amber, how are you?" China answered the phone.

"Hey lil' sis," she replied. "Girl, I'm hanging in there."

"Amber, I'm really worried about momma. She doesn't sound so well. How is she?"

"She fine. I'm on my way there to take care of her right now."

"Okay thanks. Can you call me when you get there?"

"Sure. Love you. I will call you in ten minutes," Amber replied.

"Love you too. Bye," China said.

China felt a sigh of relief. But, she also was concerned that her sister, Amber would not follow through. That's why China was not surprised when she did not call her back in the ten minutes.

China got home and noticed her handsome husband sitting on the couch waiting for her. "Hey honey," she said, placing her brief case on the counter top.

"Hey babe," he replied.

"Here are left overs," she handed him the bag.

"Thanks," he immediately took the bag and began to eat the steak. "How was your day?" he asked, chewing and talking simultaneously.

"Busy. I got a call from my mom and I'm a little worried about her. I think I'm going to have to travel home to check on her."

"Let me know what I can do."

China watched Cory eat the steak. He looked up at her. He dropped the fork and caressed his wife. They made love to sleep.

China's phone rang at 2 am. It was Amber. "Hello," China answered the phone.

"Hey lil' sis." Amber said, crying on the phone.

"What's wrong Amber?"

"Momma had a heart attack. She's in the hospital. Come home now China."

Chapter Seven

IT WAS A FALL SATURDAY in 1998. China and her siblings buried their mom next to her and Tena's father. Even though their family lived completely separate lives, they were bonded and close. They loved each other very much.

During the repass, China was comforted by school time friends that she hadn't seen since she departed New Berry. There was this one man looking at China the entire time. He looked familiar, but China could not remember exactly who he was. The guest started to leave. The man, sat there not really consoling anyone.

"Hey Nubia." China paused.

"Yeah?" she responded.

"Do you know who that man is?" China asked, gesturing towards the stranger.

"No. I wonder who he is."

The man could sense that the family was starting to wonder who he was. He began to walk toward the family.

"Hey new girl," the man said. It was Ray Ray, Crawl's friend from back in the day.

"Oh my goodness," China said surprisingly. "Ray Ray, is that you?"

"Me in the flesh." He replied, giving China a hug. "I'm so sorry about your mom. She really looked out for us."

China stared at Ray Ray. He had gray hair and looked to be in his fifties instead of his twenties. "Thank you," she replied. "How have you been?"

Ray Ray replied in a strange tone, "You will know soon enough."

China was totally blown off by his response. She began to wonder, what could he be talking about? She hadn't seen Ray Ray since high school graduation.

China and her family left the repass and went to their mother's home to have a sleep over.

"Good morning Babe. How are you feeling?" Cory asked China.

"I'm okay. I really miss momma. I miss her phone calls. I miss her so badly." She began to cry.

"I know babe." Cory tried consoling his wife. "It'll get better, I promise." He kissed her on the forehead.

"I know you have to leave. I'm going to stay here a few days to be with my sisters. I'll be fine."

"Are you sure? You know that I'm here if you need me no matter what."

"I know honey. I think it would be better for me and my sisters to be here for each other. I know that you are a phone call away."

"Okay. I'll book a flight for this evening."

"Okay," China replied.

China was leaving the airport from dropping Cory off, she began to wonder about Ray Ray's comments. She pulled up to her mother's house and began to walk in when Ray Ray walked up behind her, "so, new girl?"

China turned and replied, "Ray ray, I think you can cut it with the new girl bit."

"You right," Ray Ray replied, giggling holding his hand over his mouth.

"What's going on Ray Ray?"

"You tell me. You the one who did dirt and act like nothing happened all these years?"

"What on earth are you talking about? I haven't done anything."

"Oops my bad. Did I say dirt? I meant Dirty. My, how some people forget how *DIRTY* they used to be," he said, smugly.

"Cut the small talk. If you are trying to reference specifics to me do so or move on," she replied in an angry tone.

"Year 1988, Maura, Crawl, Dirty. Do I need to keep going?"

"You can keep going straight to hell because I don't know what you are talking about." She walked away heading into her mother's house.

"Well let's see if the New Berry P.D. will remember what I'm talking about." He walked away. "You have until 1pm tomorrow to remember. 1 pm."

China had a back flash. She remembered when Maura told her to return to her apartment at 11 pm years ago. She began to worry greatly. She thought, *every time I come to this town, I have to live in torment over what happened almost ten years ago.* She knew that she didn't do anything to get in trouble. Maura was the one that killed Dirty. She didn't have anything to worry about.

China could not sleep at all that evening. She was remembering that evening when Maura hit Dirty with the beer bottle. Ray Ray was nowhere in sight. Maybe Maura got out of jail and told him. *How on earth could he possibly know anything about that evening,* she thought. She decided that there was no way that she was going to meet Ray Ray at 1 pm. She would not leave the house to run into him. All of this would just go away.

The next morning, China and her sisters made breakfast in their mother's kitchen. They were remembering how their mother would put sugar in their oatmeal. They used to think it was so good. They were laughing saying that they wouldn't dare to put sugar in oatmeal now. They couldn't believe how much they had changed. While they sat at the kitchen table, China began to think about the past. The thought about Dirty and the threat of Ray Ray. She tried to question her sisters to see if she could get anything out of them about what had happened almost ten years ago in the building across the street. "So do you all remember the doctor's store?" she asked.

"Yeah," answered Alexa. "They had the best strawberry cookies."

"Those were the good ole days," Donte added.

"So, I wonder what happened to all the people that lived in that now, abandoned building." China said openly.

"They all moved away, except for Maura." Amber said.

"Who is Maura?" China asked as if she had no idea who she was.

"She was the hooker that was out all night. You remember her don't you? Everybody knew Maura." Amber added.

"Hooker? Are you talking about that lady that was getting in all those cars with all her different boyfriends?" China asked.

They all laughed. And when China thought about it, she couldn't help but laugh too.

"Wow. You know, I'm just realizing, that lady was a hooker. I just thought she had a lot of boyfriends. How naïve was I?" China said. "I wonder if she is still doing that."

"She went to jail for killing that boy. Yawl remember?" Tena said, sipping a cup of tea.

"Really?" China asked, "she actually killed somebody?"

"Yep," replied Amber. "It was that boy that used to run up behind you. What was his name?"

"Crawl," responded Tena.

"Yes. That's his name. Crawl," Amber said.

China could not believe what she was hearing. *How could Maura be in jail for killing Crawl? They have to have the names mixed up. Maura killed*

Dirty. Something was not adding up," she China. Something's were just not adding up.

After breakfast, all the sisters wanted to look at pictures to remember their childhood and their mother. They sat in the living room going reminiscing. The doorbell rang.

"I'll get it." China headed to the door. When she saw that it was Ray Ray, she began to feel nervous in her stomach. She thought, he can't know anything. She would just deny his allegations and see what he has to say. "It's that man Ray Ray from last night. I wonder what he wants."

She opened the door and Ray Ray stood there looking at China with a smirk on his face.

"What brings you here today, Ray Ray?" she asked him, looking directly in the eyes.

"I was just checking to see if you ladies were okay. Your mom always looked out for us. I thought I would repay her gestures."

"We are fine. Thank you for stooping by." China began to close the door. Ray Ray stopped the door from closing all the way. He gave China a paper with a phone number on it. China crumpled the paper and threw it outside and closed the door. She thought the only way to show this individual that he could not scare her was to be tough and ignore the message he was trying to say. She figured if she does not take into it, this whole thing would once again go away. She also could not help but wonder what he thought he had on her.

The next day, China went to the New Berry Library to find news clippings from the Crawl murder, and to see if there was anything on Dirty. When she arrived at the Library, she could not believe how much it had changed with the new technology. There was even a computer. She began to pull the newspaper articles for June, 1988. She came across an article dated June 23, 1988, *Local Woman Kills Under-aged Boyfriend in Love Triangle.* China could not believe what she was reading. *Maura*

Michaels 34 killed Darren Rogers also known as "Crawl" in result of lovers quarrel. China was in complete shock. *"This could not be true,"* she thought. The paper goes on to state that there was another man and under aged boy on the scene as well. They did not mention the other names in the article.

All China could think was, *why would Maura kill Crawl. Who else was there and what happened to Dirty's body?* There was only one way to get to the bottom of it.

China had to find a way to talk to Maura. She began to research related articles about Maura Michaels. She was also thinking to herself, the last name Michaels sounded familiar. She found a news article that said that Maura plead guilty to involuntary manslaughter and was sentenced to 15 years in prison. She was scheduled to be released in 2000, with good behavior. China had to try and pay her a visit before she returned home to Caryville. She wrote down the name of the prison that Maura was in and left the library.

That evening China was up all night. She knew that things were off from that night she remembered. She had never visited anyone in jail before. That was another reason that she could not sleep.

Chapter Eight

CHINA REACHED THE PRISON TO visit Maura.

"State the name of the prisoner," the prison guard ordered.

"Maura Michaels," she answered, nervously.

"Place your I.D. in the pocket."

China placed her Tennessee Driver's License in the window pocket. The guard ran her information in a computerized data base. China signed her name on paperwork. She was then escorted through a steel door. She was asked to empty her pockets and walk through an X-ray machine. Then she was escorted into a waiting lounge.

After 30 minutes of waiting, the door opened and Maura walked in the room. She looked very old. Her hair was gray and she had gained a lot of weight. Maura looked up and asked China, "You waiting for me?"

"Yes Maura," she replied.

"Who are you? How do you know my name?"

"I used to live in the house across the street from the apartment building you lived in. I came to your house with Crawl that night you went to jail. Crawl called me Lil' momma. Do you remember?"

Maura looked in China's eyes and tears began to fall down her cheeks.

"Maura, why are you crying? What's wrong?"

"Why did you come here girl?" she wept.

"I read a news article that said that you were in jail for killing Crawl. I was confused. I came down here to find out if it was true?"

"It happened just how the paper said it happened. That's all I got to say about it." Maura said bluntly. She began to walk away.

"Wait Maura." China insisted, "I need your help. There's this guy named Ray Ray..."

Before China could get another word out, Maura turned around and asked, "Ray Ray? What about Ray Ray? Do you know him? When did you talk to my son?"

"Oh my goodness Maura. Is Ray Ray your son?" China asked in disbelief.

"Yes, that is my only son. I haven't seen him in seven years. When did you see him? How is he? Do you know how I can get in touch with him?"

"Hold on Maura, I am trying to take all this in. Are you telling me that Ray Ray is your son?"

"Yes, girl. He is my son."

"Does Ray Ray know what happened the night you killed, well you know who?"

"I can't say anything else until I talk to Ray Ray. Do you know how I can reach him?"

"I don't. He still lives by my mother's house. He's asking me questions and trying to get me to say things. Do you know anything about why he's trying to say things to me about that night?"

"Listen girl, I'm due to get out of here in two months. I need to talk to Ray Ray. If you get him to come here this week, I'll tell you everything you ask. Get him down here please," she insisted as she walked away crying.

The drive back to China's mother's house was silent. China was feeling like she was living in the twilight zone. When she got back to New Berry and walked in her mom's house, her sisters were waiting.

"Hey girl. Where have you been all day?" Donte asked.

"Oh, I went to see an old acquaintance. That's all. What are we doing tonight?" China asked to change the subject quickly.

"Well, after you call that husband of yours back," Amber paused, "he called you three times. Maybe we can go out to eat or to the Moonlight Lounge."

"Okay. Let me call Cory. Excuse Me." China replied.

"Hello," Cory answered the phone.

"Hey Honey," China responded. "How was your day?"

"Hey sweetheart. I have been calling you all day. Did your sisters tell you I called?"

"Yes. I just got back from visiting an old acquaintance. I'll tell you all about it when I get back next week."

"Next week?" he said, "I thought you were coming back this weekend?"

"I was intending to. But, we have a few more loose ends to tie up. I promise I'll make it up to you when I get back."

"I want to get on a plane and come back there. I'm missing you too much."

"You do not know how much I want to get out of here. But, you understand don't you?"

"Yes, babe, I understand. Take as much time as you need. But, please don't let it be more than next week," he laughed.

"Oh, it won't I promise. I love you,"

"I love you more. Have a good night."

"You too. Bye." China hung up the phone.

After China hung up the phone, she still needed more time to digest all that she had discovered that day. Maura killed Crawl. Ray Ray is Maura's son. She did not know how much else she could take. China knew that if she didn't go out with her sisters that they would think something was wrong. She took a shower and got dressed. She went out with her sisters.

Amber decided the club that they went to. There weren't many clubs in town. The sisters went downtown Chicago to a sports bar that played live band instead of the night lounge. When they arrived, there were a lot of people at the bar. China and her sisters ordered drinks and sat at the table listening to the band. Amber asked China to go to the bar to get her another beer. China ordered the beer. While she was waiting, Ray Ray appeared out of nowhere.

"So, you just not going to make me happy are you?" he asked.

"I saw your mother this morning. She would like for you to go see her." China replied. She grabbed her sister's beer off the bar and walked away.

Ray Ray was speechless.

That night China didn't sleep at all. She thought, *Why was this happening to me? I really wish my mother was here to straighten this mess out; or at least help me make sense out of it.*

The next morning China got dressed and got in her rental car. She decided to see if she could find Ray Ray to see if his attitude had changed since he now knows that she knew who his mother was. She also wanted to see if she could pry more information from him to see exactly what he think he knew. She drove around the blocks by her mother's house, but Ray Ray was nowhere to be found. She went to the soul food restaurant, grabbed lunch for her sisters and returned to her mother's house.

"Welcome back run-a-way Susie. Where have you been again? You better stop running off like that girl. We are worried about you." Nubia said.

"I'm sorry, I went to grab lunch, see." China replied trying to change the subject quickly. It worked, her sisters grabbed the bags and ate happily.

"While you were gone, Ray Ray came by looking for you again. What is all of that about? He know you married right?" Donte asked.

"Yes, he knows I'm married. It's not that. He just keep trying to rehash how his friend that died used to like me. I'm so over that past life. I wish he would move on. I'm trying to be nice, that's all," she replied.

"He left his beeper number. It's by the phone. He said to page him when you get back," said Donte.

China finished her meal. She took the piece of paper with the beeper number and put it in her pocket. She paged Ray Ray.

The phone rang. "Hello, did someone page Ray Ray?"

"Ray Ray, this is China. We need to talk. Meet me at New Berry Mall at 5 sharp, in front of the Shoemart. Bye," she hung up the phone, not allowing Ray Ray a chance to respond.

"Nubia, I have to run out to grab more underwear. I didn't plan to stay this long and did not bring enough," she said. She picked up her purse and car keys.

"Well, I need to grab JJ new shoes. I'll go with you," Nubia replied.

China couldn't tell her sister no, or she would know that something was going on. They arrived at the mall. China began to come up with plans to separate from Nubia to meet Ray Ray.

"Nubia, I'm going to Secrets, I will meet you at the Shoemart when I am done," she said.

"Okay, I'll be in the kids shoe section."

China ran to Secrets, grabbed a few garments and began to head toward the Shoemart. She heard someone hissing at her. She turned and there was Ray Ray in the corner signaling for her to come near him. China walked towards Ray Ray and pointed for him to walk towards the end of the strip of the mall.

"I have a message for you," China said.

"A message, from who?"

"One, Ms. Maura Michaels." Ray Ray's smirk turned into a droop.

"What's wrong, momma's baby, not so tough after all."

Ray Ray grabbed China by the face and pushed her head against the wall. She kneed him in his groin. He let her go and fell to the ground. China looked up to see if anyone saw what was happening. It was clear. She kneeled over him and whispered, "Don't you ever come for me like that. You have no idea who I am."

"I know exactly who you are. You are a murderer." He grunted, holding his groin area.

"I've never killed anyone. Ask your mother about that. By the way, she is getting out in two months. She wants you to come and see her before she gets out. Are we good? Or do I need to go back to yo mommy and tell her that you had a bad accident," she said, in a threatening tone.

"Is that a threat?" he said, still in the kneeling position.

"Oh I didn't threaten anyone. But, if you think you have something on me, you need to put it behind you. You have nothing. I'm not sure what your mother told you about what happened the night she went to jail. But, it's a lie if you think I had anything to do with it." China said as she began to walk away.

Chapter Nine

"WELCOME TO BUCKNER REALTY. I'M certain that we will find the home of your dreams." China welcomed her new clients to her office. They researched the real estate data base for potential homes. Her clients were interested in three. China handed them an outline of their selections.

"Shall we?" China said, and she opened the door for them to depart for the viewings.

They approached China's car. She looked up and noticed a woman standing at the end of the block. It was Maura. *How on earth did Maura find her,* she thought. *What was she doing in Caryville? What was she doing in Tennessee?* She and her clients proceeded to the viewings.

After the showings, they returned to the office and her clients left in their car. China went into her office. She asked the receptionist if she had any messages. She went through them. There was one from someone that claimed to be looking for a new home. The person was moving from Illinois, and left the name Rogers. China fell down in her office chair with her face in her hands, in disbelief. She knew it had to be from Maura. She threw the message in the garbage, and headed home for the evening.

"Hey Honey." China greeted Cory when she arrived home.

"Hey sweetheart. How was your day?" he asked.

"Busy as usual," she kissed him on the lips. "How was your day?"

"It was busy as well. I checked the house messages when I was in between rounds at the hospital, Nubia left a message. She said for you to call her when you can."

"Oh, Lord, I hope everything is okay. Let me call her back right now. Oh, I picked up Chinese Food," she said, and pointed to the kitchen counter.

"Hey sis. How are you?" China asked Nubia after Nubia answered her telephone.

"I'm okay. How are you?"

"I'm fine. I'm returning your call. Is everything okay?"

"Yes. Everything's fine. I called you to tell you that I'm having a 40th birthday party. Can you make sure that your schedule is clear, Miss Busy Boo?"

"Cory and I definitely will make it. Your birthday falls on a Thursday this year. What day will the party be on?"

"Oh, it'll be Saturday, the twenty-fifth. I'm glad you'll make it. I miss you sis."

"I miss yawl, too. We'll see yawl in a couple of months."

"Okay. Bye, love you."

"Love you too, bye," China replied.

"Cory, Nubia is having a 40th birthday party. I told her that we'll attend. Check your schedule at work and let me know so that I can book our flights."

"Will do. I'll let you know by tomorrow."

China soaked in the bath tub. She couldn't help but think about Maura's appearance at her office earlier that day. *What could these people want with me? Why are they continuing to bother me?* She thought, *I'm not some naïve kid from New Berry. I have to deal with this matter and end it.*

"Buckner Realty, China speaking how may we serve you?" China answered her office phone.

"Hey babe, just wanted to call you, and let you know that I won't be able to go to Nubia's party, after all." Cory greeted her.

"That's fine, honey. I understand. What's going on that weekend in doctor land?" she asked and smiled though the phone.

"That weekend is the Doctors Alliance Medical Conference. The hospital already selected the attending physicians and my name is on the list. The conference is very important to my career. What if I buy Nubia a great present? Do you think she would forgive me?"

"Honey, don't worry about her party. I am definite she'd understand. It's probably going to be mostly women, anyway. I only wish I could attend the conference with you myself. Hey, maybe we can get her two, really nice presents," they both laughed hysterically.

"Okay, babe. I'll see you later. Have a great day. Love you."

"Love you, too. Bye." She said, and hung up the phone.

"Mrs. Jackson, you have a customer waiting." The receptionist announced over the intercom.

China double checked her calendar. She didn't see anyone scheduled. She called the receptionist. "Charlotte, is it a walk-in? I don't have anyone scheduled today."

"No, ma'am. It's the client that stopped by yesterday afternoon, when you were out with the Carsons. She said she was in the area again, and wanted to know if you could see her today."

"Thanks, Charlotte. I'll be out in a minute."

China grabbed her pad and pen. She walked to greet the client. She was so hoping it was a new client, and not Maura. However, when she reached the reception area, she found out it was Maura.

"Welcome to Buckner Realty. How may we serve you," China asked.

"Hi, Miss. I'm looking for a house in this city, and wanted to know if you could help me," Maura replied.

"I'd be more than happy to help. Come with me, please." She guided her to the conference room.

"Maura, what on earth are you doing in Caryville? Are you lost?"

"I am. I'm HOPING you will help me find my way."

"Maura, what do you want. You know good and well that you don't want a house."

"I want what you owe me, missy. I want my money for the time I lost in that jail."

"I have no idea what you're talking about. Are you on medication? Do I need to call you a doctor?"

"You got that right. You can start with that doctor husband of yours. When you call him, you may as well tell him that you helped me do that thing back in the day."

"Lady, now I know that you're crazy. I didn't help you do anything. You can't prove anything. You and your crack head son better stop bothering me. I ain't that little missy poo, I used to be. You don't want to mess with me. How on earth did you find out where I was anyway?"

"Who do you think you talking to, gal? You think you bad? Try me. I want twenty-five thousand, cash by next week, or you going down. And it don't matter how I found you. I got my ways. I'm coming back here in seven days. Have my money, or else."

"Ma'am, you can come back in seven days, or seventy days. I ain't given you a dime. I didn't do anything. Do what you got to do. Matter fact, don't bring your crooked tail back to my office. I'll inform the receptionist that you have changed your mind, and that I'm not interested in you as a client. If you come back here, you will be in jail. Hey aren't you on parole? You are not even supposed to be out of Illinois. Good bye, birdie. If you come anywhere near me, I'll take the office tape to the Illinois Sheriffs, and send your tale right back up the river. You must like water. Get the hell out of here." She walked Maura to the door.

"Sorry we couldn't help you, miss. Safe travels."

On the ride home China begin to think and hoped that Maura was scared off. She thought, *no telling where, or if Ray Ray was in town. I have to be on alert. I definitely have to finish this fiasco when I get back to New Berry for Nubia's party.* She made plans to stay there for the whole week.

Chapter Ten

"PARTY TIME!" CHINA SAID. SHE surprised her sisters awaiting her arrival. Nubia picked her up from the airport.

All the sisters gathered for a group hug. They really loved each other.

"Oh, my. I've missed yawl so much," China cried. "Uhm, who's cooking?" she smelled an aroma from the kitchen.

"That's Donte burning up her master '*soul food*' recipes," Tena whispered.

Donte heard Tena's comments and said, "don't act like I can't cook. My man eats my food ev-ery night." They all laughed.

"Donte it's okay. We all know yo' food is the bomb," China said, and they all more. "I was telling Nubia that I ordered a cake for her from New Berry Bakery. What else do we have to do for the shin-dig?"

"Well, yawl know I could cook most of the food, right?" Donte said, and they all looked at each other, and laughed more.

"Thanks. Sis. But, this is my 40th. Relax. Let's have it catered. Okay? You can cook for China's birthday next month." Nubia said. China looked at Nubia, surprised. They laughed, again.

China went up to her mother's room, now, her new guest room. She began to cry, and remembered her mom sitting on the bed. Amber had left her mother's room the same. She hadn't changed the sheets or anything else.

China pulled the sheets off the bed to wash them. She noticed a bulge in the bed between the mattress and the base board. She lifted the mattress, and there was a plastic bag with papers in them. She was in awe. She wondered if she should call her sisters so that they could look through the bag together. But, she decided not to. She didn't want to upset anyone if it was bad news that their mom was hiding. She decided to wash the sheets first, and then after dinner talk to her sisters about the papers.

Dinner was great. The sisters told Donte that they thought she prepared a wonderful meal. They remembered their mother, and completed plans for Nubia's party.

China took a bath, and then called Cory to say good night. "Hey, honey. How was your day?" she asked.

"Hello, my love. Aside from missing you, everything's fine. How are things going back home? And how are the Bartson Sisters?"

"Everyone's great. We're really enjoying our time together," China replied. They talked for about 30 minutes, and wished their love and good nights.

China didn't mention anything about the papers she had discovered after dinner as she had planned. She didn't want to take the moment she and her sisters were sharing about their late mother for granted.

China sat on her mom's bed, and began to open the papers. It looked like some type of insurance policy. It was dated August 1, 1990 by a Clarence Earrins. The beneficiary was Emma Barston, China's mother. Mr. Earrins left China's mother fifty thousand dollars. China couldn't believe what she was reading. She wondered, *who was Clarence Earrins, and why had he left her mother so much money.* There was another paper at the bottom of the stack of papers. It was a letter addressed to China's mother. It stated that Clarence Earrins claimed to be the biological father of Nubia and Amber. He left the money to them, in care of their mother. China wondered, *do my sisters know about the policy, and what had momma done with the money.* She had to tell them about it.

"Good morning Barstons," China said, and she walked in the kitchen. All of her sisters were at the table. Nubia was cooking pancakes.

"So, what's the plan for today?" Nubia asked.

"Well, I think we all need to talk for a minute. Last night I was changing the sheets in momma's room, and I felt a budge sticking between the mattress and box spring. It was an insurance policy to momma from someone claiming to be Nubia and Amber's father."

"Oh, we know about it. Momma had it for some time. We never really knew Mr. Earrins, but, good looking out," Nubia said.

"How can you be so vein about it? Are you guys okay? And what happened to all that money?"

"Girl, we're fine. That was years ago. Momma explained everything to us. We understand. The money? Well, momma used it for the needs of this place. She also used some for your college tuition. So, no worries. That's old news. Momma did what she had to do," Nubia said.

China noticed Amber looking at her with this bland look on her face. China was only imagining what Amber was thinking.

"What's wrong, Amber? Are you okay?" China asked.

"Gir,l I'm fine, just fine," she walked slowly out of the kitchen.

China began to think about how she used to wonder how her mother got the rest of the money for her tuition. She never thought to ask about it, because she was carefree.

China decided to go check on the cake order in person to make sure the designer had everything on the cake as China explained. She didn't want errors to the cake from missed communication. She walked to Nubia's car, looked up, Ray Ray and Maura stood at the car looking at her. China felt nervous, because she felt like there were going to attack her.

"We in my town now, Miss know it all. What you gone do now?" Maura asked. China backed away, because she felt that Maura was trying to fight her.

"Ray Ray and Maura, why do yawl keep bothering me. I told yawl I haven't done anything. I told yawl, I'm not giving yawl one red cent. I told yawl, that you could run, and tell who ever all want. You have nothing on me. Stop the games. Get this over with."

"You can kill it with the threats. We aint going to the cops. We going straight to the good doctor. How would he like to hear 'bout his wife killing an innocent being? I'm sure he wouldn't be too happy?" Ray Ray continued, "what you think momma? Do you think the doc. would welcome his queen back with opened arms when he finds out she a bad ass?"

"I'm with you Ray Ray. He gone dump this bimbo. Maybe he would rather have this real deal after that," Maura said, and she swirled her hips in a circular motion.

"Look damn it. You can tell my husband, and you can tell the president of these United States. I don't care. You won't get a dime from me. If you keep coming for me, I'll file charges. Got it?" she said. She got in the car, and drove away.

On the ride home, China began to think, *the only way to deal with this crazies it to act crazy right along with them. If I entertain their nonsense, they'll keep at it. I have to show them that I did not care. I didn't do nothing wrong.* She also thought, *I should tell at least Nubia or Cory about this. They would know exactly what to do. I would tell Cory when I get home that there are individuals from my childhood that are making up this cockamamie story, and I'm innocent. He would believe me.*

The next day, China went to the local party decoration store to order balloons. She walked through the store. She looked up, and Maura approached her out of nowhere.

"China, I really feel bad about all of this. Everything's not how it seems. I need to tell you things."

"I'm listening."

"Not here. Not in the open like this," Maura said, and she looked around. China looked around too, to see if she could figure out what Maura was looking around at.

"Maura, what are you looking around for."

"Oh, I'm just making sure I'm not being watch. It comes with the territory."

"Okay. Meet me at New Berry Wings in one hour," China suggested.

"Girl, that is, she caught herself, that's not a good spot."

"Why not," China replied. She wasn't sure she could trust Maura.

"Let's just say, people know me there. Meet me at the library in one hour," she replied, and they both walked away.

China couldn't bring herself to trust Maura. She decided to secretly record their conversations.

China arrived at the library early to see if Maura would come with others. She parked in a corner away from view. Maura got off the bus, and walked into the library. China waited a few minutes. She drove to the library parking lot, and parked in front. She walked into the library, and Maura was sitting with a book in hand. China grabbed a book off the shelf. "Hi Maura, reading anything interesting," she asked. China knew that Maura was not truly reading the book she was holding.

"China, I'm really sorry about all of this. I'm here to help you. But, I'm really here, so you could help me. I'm so tired and afraid." Maura continued. "The night when Crawl brought you to my house, you didn't do anything, at all. When you left, we all thought that Dirty was dead. He wasn't dead. I just knocked him out when I hit him with that bottle." She went on, "thirty minutes after you left, Dirty got up, and came after me. He began to hit me in the face. Crawl jumped in. Dirty and Crawl began to fight. That's when my son, Raymond, you know him as Ray Ray, walked in the house. He saw the man he had known as his father and Crawl fighting. Crawl was on top of Dirty getting him good. Raymond put Crawl in a choke hold. Dirty got up, grabbed his gun, and shot Crawl in the head. We were all sitting there, stunned. Dirty began to put a story together for the cops. He wiped the gun off, and gave it to me. He told me to hold it. I told him no. He told me that if I didn't, that Raymond would go to jail for murder. I didn't want my son in jail. I went along with the story. I was sentenced to 15 years in jail for a deal I worked out with the prosecutor. All these years and I went to jail for something I didn't even do," tears rolled down Maura's face.

China didn't say anything. She was in awe. She cleared her throat, "I'm so sorry Maura for all of your troubles. So, Dirty was not killed, and he is Ray Ray's father?"

"Dirty is not really Raymond's father. But, he was the only father Raymond knew. I met Dirty at a very early age. I was pregnant with Raymond when I met him. My parents found out I was pregnant, and they threw me out of the house. Dirty put me up in an apartment. After I had Raymond, he put me on the streets. I had no other choice. He told me that he would throw me and Raymond out if it didn't bring money into the house. Dirty died of a drug overdose five years ago. For some reason Raymond is blaming you for me going to jail, and for Dirty's drug overdose. I tried to tell him that you had nothing to do with this whole mess. He said that if I would never have hit Dirty with that bottle, the fight between Dirty and Crawl never would have happened, and landed me in jail. I don't agree with that. I need your help to get away from Raymond, before I wind backup in jail, or before he does something to hurt you," she took a tissue out of her pocket to wipe tears from her face.

"What do you mean, hurt me?"

"China, you don't understand how serious this is. He's blaming you for everything. I mean everything that ever happened to him when I went to jail. My son is all I have in this world. I would do anything for him. I had time to think, when I was in jail. I have grown a great deal. This isn't right what he is doing. Somebody is going to get hurt. He's involved with some woman. That's how he found out that you lived in Tennessee. She knows you somehow."

"Maura, let me take all of this in. Tomorrow is my sister's party. Can you meet me here, Monday at 2pm?"

"Okay, but don't wait too long. We don't have much time," she left China sitting at the table.

China began to think that she was in the clear. She had everything on tape. But, she could not help but to think about Maura. She felt really bad for Maura. She really did not want any part of Maura or Ray Ray. She had to make Maura understand. If there was some way she could help Maura get away for Ray Ray, she would. After all, Maura did jump to her defense to save her from Dirty that night.

The day of Nubia's party was a blast. They had so much fun. For some reason, Amber was not herself. China wished that Amber would get into a drug rehab program.

The next morning, the sisters went to church and went home for dinner. "That was the best party ever. Thanks yawl so much, for everything," Nubia said.

"It sure was," Donte said. "Just think, if I would have catered the event, it would have been on the news." They all laughed.

"China, when do you leave?" Nubia asked.

"I go home Tuesday Morning. I wish I could stay longer. But, I gotta get back to my boo."

"I know that's right." Tena said, and she high-fived China.

Amber walked away to the restroom.

"So, you guys, I'm really worried about Amber," China said. "She's really been quiet, and not acting normal. I think she needs help."

"You know she on that stuff," Alexa said.

"Yes, but we need to help her. Momma isn't here to keep after her. We need to try to get her to go to rehab," China stopped talking because she noticed that Amber coming back. Everyone was quiet.

"Why yawl so quiet. Don't stop talking on my account. I ain't nobody," Amber said.

"Hey Amber, I was thinking that maybe you would like to come stay with me for a while. You know, you really haven't been outside of New Berry," China suggested.

"Girl, this is home. I don't want to go anywhere else."

"We thought that since Momma is not here anymore, that maybe you wanted to get out and see more of the world," China said. "Why don't you take some time, and think about it? Just let me know. I'll come and pick you up myself. I could even get you a job at my company."

"Thanks. But, no thanks. I have some things in the works right here, in New Berry. Ima be fine."

"Hey, did yawl see Sister Donnelson pass out in church today?" Donte said, to change the subject. "That was something. She's always getting the spirit, and they have to put somebodies funky shoe in her face to revive her. Yuck." They all laughed.

China lay in her mom's bed. She couldn't help but think about Maura. She had no idea what she was going to say to Maura. She had cash left over from her trip that she'd planned to spend on Nubia's party, which she did not use. She could give that to Maura as a gift, and hopefully Maura would accept it. China would leave, and end this ordeal. She thought how she would love to put Ray Ray in his place, and tell him that she had a confession about everything on tape. She thought, he would have no choice but to leave her alone. Then she thought about the warning that Maura told her about Ray Ray really wanting to get even with her for everything that happened during his childhood. China begin to get upset. *Why did I get so caught up in to Crawl, in the first place? Why couldn't I just put him out of my mind? If I would have stayed away from Crawl, I would never had been in this mess.*

The next afternoon, China did the same thing meeting Maura. She arrived early to the library, and waited for Maura to get off the bus. She put a new tape in the recorder, and walked into the library. Maura was wearing glasses.

"Hi Maura. How are you?" China asked, and she sat down. Maura took the glasses off. She had two black eyes. "Oh my goodness Maura, what happened?"

"I need your help. Please help me get out of here." Maura pleaded.

"Look Maura, I was thinking about all of this. This is really too much for me. Here is money that I'd saved up. I want you to have it. I hope it helps you get away, and get a new life started." China pulled an envelope from her purse, and put it inside a book. She passed it to Maura. Maura opened it up.

"Five hundred dollars? Gal, what is this going to do?"

"It's all I have, right now. I want to help you do something."

"Girl, I put my life on the line twice, no three times for you, and this all you can do? I should have let Dirty get you that night. I should have let Ray Ray keep torturing you. I came to you for help, and opened up to you because I cared about you, and this is all the help I get. I put you over my own son," Maura began to cry.

"Wait Maura. How would you like to come to Caryville? I can try to put you up in one of my vacant properties. I will pay the owners a fee to rent the homes until it's sold. You could stay there until you find some place of your own."

"Girl, are you forgetting that I'm on parole. I caint leave this state for thirty-six months. You have to come up with a better plan than that."

"What if we were to go to the police to tell them the truth about what happened that night in the apartments? Ray Ray would go to jail, and you would be free."

"Girl, are you crazy. I thought you were a college graduate. I already did time for that. I didn't want my son in jail then, and I do not want him there now. I really care about him. He's just out of his mind right now."

"Well Maura, I don't know what else to tell you." China said and she began to get up. "I really hope that you are freed from all this pain one day," she walked out the library.

When China got back to her mother's house, Amber was there sitting in the living room waiting. "Hey China. Where did you go?"

"I went to get Cory a present for when I return home. Is everything okay?" China replied.

"Yeah. I was thinking about what you said, about me getting my life together. I could use help. Momma didn't really leave any money. She left this house. You all agreed that I could keep it. I want to do things for myself. I never really knew how. I was always under momma. My father who I never knew left money, and momma used it to survive, and pay for your college. So I was thinking, the money that momma used towards your college, that you could give me some back so that I could get a fresh start."

China could not believe what she was hearing. Was her older sister asking her to return money that their mother took from an inheritance, of which, she knew nothing about, and that she had no control over?

"Okay Amber. How much were you thinking?" China asked in curiosity.

"Well the insurance policy was for fifty thousand dollars. How about twenty-five thousand?"

"I don't have twenty-five thousand dollars. Are you seriously asking me to pay you back for money that momma gave me, and that I didn't know anything about?"

"You bet I am. That money was mine. Momma had no right to use it for you."

"My goodness, Amber. It was not like you were in college or anything. If you look at it, you live in this house. Could it be possible that momma used your half towards this house that you live in for free?"

After a brief silence, Amber continued, "Oh well, you were offering yesterday, I just thought I would ask."

"I was offering you a fresh start from this place. But, now I really don't think that would be a good idea."

China felt really bad about the spat between her and Amber. She really loved sister very much. She decided to make amends. She was walking down the hall to Amber's room, and she heard Amber arguing with someone on the phone. She tried to listen in to see if she could find out what was being said. But, the words were unclear. She really began to worry about Amber. She decided that she would talk to Nubia and Alexa about it in the morning. Something was truly going on with their sister. She needed their help. China said her prayer so that God could help their family. She said a special prayer for Amber.

The next morning, China prayed again. Their mother always taught them that God heard prayers, and that when in need, to seek God in prayer, and He will answer.

Amber did not attend breakfast that morning. All the other sisters were in the kitchen when China went downstairs. "Hey, has anyone talked to Amber this morning?"

"Naw," said Donte. "She's not in her room?"

"I'm not sure. I'll go back up and check on her," China replied. She went to Amber's room, and knocked on the door. There was no answer. She opened the door. The room was a mess, and had a smell. China covered her nose, and looked around to see if she could see any signs that may help her try to figure out what her sister was going through. There wasn't much that she could tell. She opened the drawers, and she saw a book that looked like a ledger, a diary of some sort. She poked her head outside the door to make sure it was still clear. She took the book to her mother's room. She opened it. It looked like a bunch of scribble scrabble. *What on earth was this about,* China thought? She wondered if her baby nieces and nephew had gotten into the room to write in the book. She whispered, *"Lord if it ain't one thing, it's another."* She tried to make out some of the words. It looked like her sister was trying to plan something out. Exactly what, China could not figure out. Now, China really was worried. She had to try to find out what Amber was into. Instead of leaving that day as planned, China decided to stay a few more days.

China waited at the house all day until Amber returned home. She had to stay close to her to find out what was going on.

Amber returned home at four o'clock in the afternoon. She greeted Amber, "Hey Amber. I missed you all day. I was waiting to see if you wanted to go to lunch."

"Dag, can I get in the house? Why you all up in my skin like that? I don't won't no lunch. I got too much to do, to go around, and sit to eat somebodies lunch," Amber replied, and she appeared to an attitude.

"What's going on with you Amber? Talk to me. I can help."

"Help? What do you mean help? I'm good. I got to go," she snapped back. Amber ran up to her room. She was in there for 45 minutes before she came out.

China decided that she would wait, and follow Amber. She would definitely find out what was going on.

Amber didn't drive because her license was suspended for having too many DUI records. China decided to follow Amber in her rental car, which she'd rented for the day.

"Nubia, I'm going to the library to print out my return flight information. I'll be back in a few hours because while I am there, I am going to catch up on a few things from my office," China lied.

"Okay, did you want to take your nephew with you, girl?" Nubia smiled.

"Not this time. I have too much to look into." She left the house, and drove to the corner. She parked, and waited for Amber to leave the house.

At seven-thirty that evening, Amber walked out the front door. She started out walking to the next corner. China started the car. She drove a block behind Amber, as she walked. Amber turned the next block, and walked in to a bar.

China parked at the middle of the street from bar entrance. She got out of the car, and walked into the bar. The bar was playing jazz music, and there were quite a few people in it. China found a spot in the corner to try to eye search for Amber. She didn't want to be noticed. She didn't see Amber. She walked around the bar with guys rubbing their bodies against her trying to pull her to dance. She gentle rejected each of them. There was a table in the corner. She could see her sister sitting there with two other people. She slowing moved towards them. As she got closer, she began to recognize won of the people. It was Ray Ray. China backed off a little bit. There was another man sitting with them. He was a much older looking man. China couldn't make out who it was because his wasn't facing her. She walked through the crowd to try to see if she could get a glimpse. She could not get a clear glimpse without being seen. She began to think, *why was Amber sitting with Ray Ray; and what could they be talking about; and who were they sitting with.* She wondered what would happen if she just walked over to the table to bust them out. She decided to lay low.

China found an empty chair at the corner of the bar. She sat there, and watched her sister sit with no good people. A tear strolled down China's face. She felt sad, and hurt. She hurt for her sister. The bartender asked China if everything was okay and she told him yes. He handed her a napkin. It was a good thing that the bar was crowded, because China did not want to be noticed. China had to figure out what they were talking about. China waited and she watched.

Out of nowhere, Maura walked in. China's jaw could have reached her knees. Maura sat in a chair next to Amber. China knew that something was going on with them. She couldn't believe her own flesh and blood would be talking to these people who were trying to blackmail her for no good reason. She wondered if Amber knew about what was going on with the blackmail issue. She had to get out of there. She began to feel sick.

China went back to her mother's house. When she walked in Nubia was sitting on the couch.

"Hey China. Are you okay? You look like you just saw a ghost." Nubia said.

"Oh, I guess I'm just a little overwhelmed with the work I had to catch up on. I'm going to go up and lie down. I will see you tomorrow, if I don't wake up before the morning."

"Okay. Let me know if you need anything," Nubia offered.

China fell on her mother's bed in tears. She could not believe everything that was happening. She called her husband, and told him that she was going to bed early. She told him, she would call him in the morning.

She could not sleep at all. She waited for Amber to come home so that she could confront her.

China was barely asleep. She heard Amber creep in the house. She looked at the clock, and it was 2 a.m. China walked to peek through the door to watch Amber walk in her room. Amber stumbled in her room, and closed the door. China walk over to Amber's door to listen. She heard nothing. China decided to give it a rest. She went back into her mother's room, and laid in the bed stunned.

The next morning, China crawled out the bed and sat there in sadness. *What was the matter with Amber? Why is she so distant?* China walked over to Amber's door and listened again. She heard silence. China knocked on her sister's door and there was no response. She opened the door. Amber was sleep. She was so deep into her sleep that she did not even hear the knock on the door. Amber's room reeked of smoke and alcohol. The smell made China's feel nauseous. She decided not to wake Amber.

She went down to the kitchen. No one else was at her mother's house that morning. People were getting back to their daily routine. Soon China knew that she would have to return to work, and her husband as well. She had to finish this business, and get back to her life. She called Cory as promised.

"Good morning honey." China greeted Cory.

"Good morning, babe. I miss you so much. When are you coming home?"

"I'm fine. How are you?"

"Can't you tell through the phone how I am? I'm bugging badly. I need you."

"I miss you too. I just called the airlines and booked my flight for Friday. A few more days okay? It's just that my sister, Amber is not in a good place right now. I am trying to help her."

"I'm sorry baby. Take all the time you need. Is there anything I can do to help?"

"No, just be a little more patience. I promise you, I'll make it up to you," she said. "I'll call you tonight. I love you so much."

"I love you too, talk to you later." They said their goodbyes.

Amber came down the stairs and sat on the couch next to China.

"Good morning Amber," China said.

"Hey. What's up?"

"I couldn't sleep much last night. I heard you come in pretty late. Do you want to talk about it?"

"I'm a grown woman. I ain't got no kids. I ain't got no husband. I aint got no momma. I ain't got nothing. I can do those types of things. You understand?"

"I do understand. But, don't you want kids, and a husband, and don't you want a job, or something."

"There you go. Listen, when you were up there all in college and things, I was here taking care of yo' momma. I was here trying to hold things down. So, don't come at me like I aint doing nothing. I have reasons for who I am. I am good." Amber began to get defensive.

"I am just trying to ask you questions. I appreciate everything that you've done for OUR mother. But, momma isn't here anymore. There is a whole world out there. My offer still stands if you want to come back to Tennessee with me. I can help you."

"Help me? Help Amber? Girl, Amber don't need nobodies help. Amber is fine." She said as she began to walk away.

"If Amber is soooo fine, why is she hanging at the clubs with nobodies?"

Amber stopped. She turned around, and looked at China, and asked, "what are you talking about?"

"I saw you last night at the club sitting with Maura and her son. What was that all about, Amber?"

"Are you spying on me?" Amber shouted.

"Girl, why are you yelling? Ain't no body spying on you? I went there last night to relax, and I saw you there. I was going to join you until I saw Maura walk in," China lied.

"Who I hang with, and who I talk to is none of your business."

"Amber, those people are not good people. You don't have any business with them. They are super crazy!" China's voice got louder.

"Well, they are there for me. When everybody keep trying to put me down, and ex-me out, they are really with me."

"Amber, we are here for you. We always have been. No one is ex-ing you out. That does not make any sense. If I only could tell you what Maura and her son have tried to do to me, you would understand better. Please listen to me. Please stay away from them. I love you Amber, despite what you may think," she pleaded.

"It's a little too late for all this love. I'm out."

"Girl, where are you going?"

"I AM GROWN!" Amber yelled back.

China grabbed Amber by the arms to try to prevent her from leaving the house. Amber slapped China across the face. She hit her so hard, China thought she was hit with a brick or something. China lost balance, and fell to the floor. She begin to scream and cry. She jumped up. She and Amber began to tussle. They were fighting, screaming, and crying.

Nubia walked in from the back door. She heard the screams through the kitchen, "HEY! STOP IT! ARE YAWL CRAZY?" Nubia yelled so that the both of them could hear.

Nubia was able to break them apart. They both were crying. Their hair was all over their heads, and one the floor.

"Now, momma would turn over in her grave if she knew about this mess. What the heck is going on?" Nubia asked.

"This psycho attacked me like I was the cat off the streets. She is completely out of her mind. She needs help." China screamed, breathing hard to catch her breath.

"Yawl gone see psycho. All these years yawl stole from me. All these years, nobody cared for me." Amber cried. She started to walk out the door, when Donte and Tena walked in the house.

"What in the world is going on up in here?" Donte asked. They all circled around Amber to stop her from leaving the house.

"Why are yawl trying to attack me? Leave me alone. Get out of my way," Amber cried as she fell to the floor. They all fell to the floor with her. They all cried, and hugged each other.

"Amber, we have to talk about this. Please let us help you. We love you so much," China cried.

The sisters collectively persuaded Amber to seek professional help.

Chapter Eleven

"GOOD MORNING BABE," CORY SAID to China while he watched her wake. "I have missed you so much." They kissed.

"I missed you too sir," she replied. They made love.

They got dressed. The sat at the kitchen table drinking coffee. "Do you have any meetings this evening after work?" Cory asked.

"Nope. What's the plan?"

"I'll figure something out. Don't make any new plans. You are booked for this very important client beginning, 6 pm sharp. Okay?"

"Meeting confirmed. Have a great day honey. Love you," she said, and they walked out of the house.

China arrived at her office, and the office receptionist greeted her, "Good morning, Mrs. Jackson. Welcome back."

"Good morning Charlotte. It's great to be back. Thank you."

"Here are your messages." Charlotte responded, and she handed China a stack of message memos. "Also, you have a showing at 10:30 am in Aurora at the Lent Estate."

"Awesome. Thank you very much." She took the messages and walked to her office.

China started her day checking her emails, and returning calls. She also ran a report of the Lent Estate so that she could be well informed about the property prior to showing it.

China arrived at the location early. She walked through the house to familiarize herself with it.

She returned to the foyer of the front entrance to await the client. The door bell sounded. China walked to the door to greet them. She was stunned to see who was at the door. It was Dirty, Maura's pimp from back in the day. China backed away from the door. Dirty pushed the door open and walked in the house. Maura and Ray Ray were with him.

"What are yawl doing here? And Maura, you told me that Dirty died. What's going on?"

"Now, that's no way to welcome friends from your home town, now is it?" Dirty replied.

"You are not dead after all?" China asked.

"You really are smart. Enough with the questions. I am here to get what you owe me," he said. Maura and Ray Ray just stood next to him in silence.

"I don't owe you anything. Now yawl need to leave, now," She said, trying not to show fear.

"You really don't get it do you? Do you know how much money you cost me all of these years? Maura was sent to jail because of your smart mouthed ass. If you would have behaved, Ray Ray here, would not have had to kill Crawl, and my money would not have spent all those years in jail. You need to pay up, or you next."

"Yawl have been bothering me for years now. I told Maura and Ray Ray that I had nothing to do with those events in the past, and that they are not my fault. Now leave before I call the cops."

Dirty laughed. He reached in his pocket, and pulled out a gun. "Go ahead, call them. What? You don't sound so brave now. As I understand it, you are married to a wealthy doctor. Now, I want a hundred thousand dollars by Monday, or forget us telling Doc all about your troubles, bang, bang, you dead. I still get headaches from the blow to the head that you caused." He said, rubbing the top of his head.

"Why is it a hundred thousand dollars now? Ray Ray said twenty-five thousand?"

"It was twenty-five thousand, before you sent your sister to the nut house before she could help us finish what we started. We have incurred additional expenses that you have to pay now. We need money now for hotel." Dirty said, and he grabbed China's purse off the table. He took all the cash she had in her wallet and dropped the wallet on the floor. China could not say, or do anything at that moment.

"See you back here at 9:00 am on Monday Morning. Be here or be dead." Dirty said as he rubbed his hand down the side of China's face. He giggled and walked out the house.

China was extremely afraid and worried. She thought, *Why on earth are these people still after me? Why is Dirty still alive? Why is my life in such a mess? I have to take things into my own hands. I can't keep letting these fools bother me like this.*

China went back to her office to think. She started to think if she went the police, they would not have any evidence that these people were trying to kill her. She needed proof. She thought if she told her husband, that he would not trust her anymore. She thought if she told her sisters that they would be more worried than she was. She had to handle it on her own. She definitely was not going to pay the money.

"Mrs. Jackson, Mr. Jackson is on line three." Charlotte said on the office intercom.

"Hey honey. How is your day going?" China said, unexcitedly.

"What's wrong, sweetheart. You sound down." Cory replied.

"Oh, I'm okay just catching up at work. What's up?"

"I'm just calling to make sure that you still have me in your book for this evening."

China was so mind boggled. But she could not let her husband down. "You are down. In fact, I'm leaving here right now to head home to get ready for ya. I will see you at home." China said, and she hung up the phone. She remained at her office another hour before leaving. She was in such a shock.

China arrived home and opened the door. There were candles, and rose peddles everywhere. Her man was standing in the middle of the living room with two glasses of wine. She dropped her purse and brief case on the floor. She rushed to her husband's arms. They shared a kissed.

"Hold on babe, I got this." Cory took China by the hand and led her to the dining room table where a fully prepared dinner awaited. They ate. He then took her up stairs, and they soaked in the bubble bath Jacuzzi. He dried her off, carried her to their bed, and massaged her body gently. They made love.

The next morning, China began doing research. She needed to figure out a way to get proof to the police that Dirty and his gang were trying to blackmail her. She went to the local shopping center and bought a tape recorder. She put together a plan that was sure to land Dirty right in jail where she thought he needed to be. She would meet him at the house. She would hide the recorder out of sight so that she could get him to repeat everything. She only had a problem with thinking of an excuse to why she didn't bring money with her. She figured if she showed him some money that he would trust her for the remaining money he was asking her for. She went to the bank, and withdrew five thousand dollars.

That whole week, China plotted and planned. She went to the house that Wednesday to setup the audio equipment in a hiding spot. She found a spot behind the plant that was in the living room. She had to somehow walk Dirty and his crew into the living room area. She planted knives in separate sections of the house so that she could grab them just in case anything went wrong. She was ready to get these people out of her life once and for all.

Chapter Twelve

THE DOORBELL RANG. "COME IN. I have your money in here." China yelled through the closed door. The door slowly opened. China only heard one set of footsteps. She looked up, and Dirty was alone.

"Where is Maura and Ray Ray?" she asked nervously.

"What are you scared of the big, bad wolf? They are at the hotel. We can do this alone. Where my money?"

"I want to be clear why you are telling me to pay you all this money. I didn't do anything. You have no reason to threaten and harass me like this."

"It's simple, you caused my money to stop coming in, and you owe me, with interest. So pay up."

"How did I stop your money from coming in? What money are you talking about, Dirty?"

"You know good and well what money I'm talking about. You are not seventeen any more. Now pay up before this gets real ugly."

"What would happen to me if I don't pay you the money you are asking me for?"

Dirty pulled the gun out of his coat pocket and waved it, and said, "Guess."

"Well, I had a problem getting all the money. It's a lot. I have some, just to buy me a little more time to come up with the rest." China picked up an envelope from the table, and handed it to Dirty.

"Girl, what the hell is this?" Dirty yelled as he threw the money on the floor. "This ain't no damn show and tell. I gave yo' ass a whole week to get my money. Now where is it?"

"I told you, I need more time. It is not easy to get a hundred thousand dollars in cash." she replied, and she began to move around the coffee table to create distance.

She could tell that Dirty was extremely upset. The plan was not going so well. She expected Maura and Ray Ray to be with him, so that she was not be alone with the crazy.

"So, you want a little more time? Okay, I will give you a little more time. That will cost you. Get over here, and pay for the extension." Dirty said, holding the gun, taking off his coat, and unbuckling his pants.

"I just need one more week Dirty, please. I promise I will have all of you money. I promise." China began to cry.

They were circling around the coffee table. Dirty threw the coffee table over, and grabbed China. He threw her on the floor. She tried to fight him off, but he was too strong. He pulled her skirt up, striped her panties down and brutally tried to go inside her. She cried and screamed for him to stop. She thought about the knives she had planted throughout the house the week before. There just happened to be one under the couch right where she lay. She reached, grabbed the knife and quickly stabbed Dirty in the neck while his face was hovered over hers. His movement halted. Blood gushed out of his neck quickly. The gun fell to the floor. Dirty's whole body flopped on top of China's.

China pulled her body from under Dirty's, and crawled to grab the gun. She pointed the gun at Dirty and pulled the trigger; but the gun was empty. She kicked him and he didn't move. She checked for a pulse and there was nothing. She cried profusely.

China thought to call the police. She then thought she had to make sure that the proof was there. She ran to the recorder that she planted. She pushed the rewind button. The tape stopped quicker than it should have. China pushed the play button. The only thing on the recording was China saying come in after the doorbell rang. The tape must have stopped recording. She had no evidence. She began to think, surely the police would understand this self-defense when the test results came back from the attempted rape. China could feel the bruises on her body. But, then she thought about the money that was on the floor. She thought it would be much surer for her to clean up the scene than to go to the police. *Nobody would miss Dirty anyway,* she thought.

China pondered about another problem, Maura and Ray Ray. Surely, they would go to the police if Dirty did not return to the hotel. She had to find out what hotel they were staying at so that she could try to see what they were up to. She rumbled through his pockets and found a hotel key for the The Caryville Inn. She grabbed it. She then emptied all his pockets. She had to clean up the house, and get the body out.

The Lent Estate was secluded. China thought that she could clean the house without anyone noticing. She had to hurry before other realtors came to show the house. She called her office, and told them that the property would be unavailable for showing the rest of the day, because she wanted to have a cleaning company clean a specific area prior to additional showings. She then called her husband and told him that she would be in showings until 8 p.m. that night.

China ran to the kitchen and grabbed plastic garbage bags and cleaning supplies. She ran to the hall closet and grabbed towels. She began to clean and scrub. She looked at Dirty's bloody, lifeless body. She began to cry again. She had to do something with it. She had no idea what. She took off her bloody clothes so that she wouldn't track blood everywhere, and make a bigger mess. She ran upstairs going through closets trying to find a big disposable bag of some sort to get the body out. The only thing that she could fine was huge comforter. *Surely his body would wrap in there,* she thought. She ran to the closet, and pulled out a women's jump suit. She put it on. She ran down stairs, and began to roll the dead body in the comforter. That didn't work. The blood began to seep through the comforter. She looked at the floor, and she a noticed rug. She wrapped Dirty's body in the rug. That worked. She took all the strength she had to pull the rug to the side door. She grabbed Dirty's keys and drove his van to the side door. She opened the back door of the van, she almost fell out when she saw what was there. It was Maura and Ray Ray, and they were dead.

China put her hands over her mouth to keep sounds from coming out. She began to cry. She had to pull it together. She pulled Dirty's body to the van. His body was too heavy. She could not get him up in the van. She rolled the rug in a horizontal position and then she climbed in the van and pulled it in the van. Dirty's feet dangled from the rug as China pulled it inside. She then ran back into the house. She ran to the living room. She grabbed all of knives, the recorder, and any other items that she or Dirty brought. She put the gun and bloody knife in her brief case. She put the money in her purse. She grabbed her clothes, and put everything else in a garbage bag. She ran those items to her car, and put them in the trunk.

China cleaned the house spotless. She thought she could call a cleaning company in the morning, and have them do a more thorough job. She looked around and the house appeared spotless. She ran to the bathroom and washed her face. The tears ran down her face. She looked in the mirror and told herself to pull it together. She ran to the van, and drove it to the back-end of the estate and parked it in the caretakers' garage. She ran back into the house to triple check the scene. She drove away in her car, and went home to clean up.

On the drive to her house, China called her husband on her car phone to make sure he was still at work. The nurse said he was in surgery, which meant that China had time to clean up, and get back to the house to move the van. She went home, took the clothes off, and showered for a whole hour. She took the knife and gun out of her briefcase, and poured bleach on them. She put the knife and gun in a paper bag, and grabbed another purse. She had to ditch them. She took the money, and put it in the house safe. She put all the clothes from the estate in a bag and grabbed everything.

China drove through alleys. She through the gun and knife in a garbage dumpster. She took the clothes to a local laundry mat, washed them, and took them to another dumpster to ditch them. She went back home wrote a note for her husband to tell him that she tried calling him while he was surgery. She wrote, that she went to a business dinner with clients, and would be home late. She told him not to wait up. She parked her car in the garage. She would answer about the car later. She grabbed business attire to change into, and then ran out of the house in her jeans and gyms shoes.

China walked to the restaurant down the street from their home and hailed a taxi. She got out the taxi at the estate and then she went through the van to make sure there was no evidence in the van. There were only dead bodies, and the van. China unwrapped the rug and comforter from Dirty's lifeless body. She put them in a hug garbage bag and put them behind the caretaker's shed to come back and retrieve later. She drove the van to the hotel to make sure there was nothing in the hotel tied to her. She had to figure out what room they were staying in. She called the hotel and asked to be connected to Michael's Room. The guest agent told her the room number she was connecting to. She went to the room, there was a suitcase and nothing else. She opened the suitcase, and went through it. There were only clothes. She grabbed the suitcase, and walked back to the van.

China began to cry as she drove around trying to decide out what to do with the bodies. There was a lake at the end of town. She drove through the forest to the lake. She wiped her fingerprints from the parts of the van she touched. She grabbed her bags out the van and threw them outside on the ground. Then she put the van in drive and took her foot off the breaks and jumped out quickly. She watched the van slowly drive into the lake. She moved the dirt around to take her footprints out the dirt.

It was starting to get dark outside. China could not think about the darkness, or walking through the woods to town. She had to hurry.

China finally made it to town. There was a bar that had a lot of cars in the parking lot. She knew that no one would notice her there. She went into the bar and she was the only black person. *Surely, I would be noticed,* she thought. She sat at the bar. She asked the bartender for a glass of moscoto.

"Hey lady, are you from 'round these parts?" The bartender asked.

"No sir. My car gave out down the road, and I walked here to wait for the taxi I just called. I walked here because I didn't want to wait on the road alone."

"Well, we aint got no wine. How 'bout a beer?"

"That'll be fine, thanks," she replied. She went to the pay phone to call a taxi. One hour later, the taxi pulled up. China got in. The taxi took her to another bar close to her house. She went in and changed clothes. She asked the bartender for a shot.

China called another taxi to take her home. When she pulled up to the house, the lights were on. She didn't have time to cry. She felt so bad. She walked in the door.

"Thank God. I was so worried. Where were you? Are you okay. How did you get home?" Cory asked question, after question.

China kissed her husband. She knew that he would be concerned, but she didn't know it would be to this extent. "I left you a note. I went to dinner with new clients. I knew I would probably drink, so I left the car home and caught a taxi home."

"I read the message but, it's eleven-thirty at night. The dinner ran that long?"

"No, afterwards we sat at the bar and socialized. These are party type clients. You know I have to entertain them to get the business done. I'm sorry. I am exhausted. Let's get some rest." She took Cory by his hands. They turned off the lights, and they went to bed.

Cory tried to make love. China pretended like she was sound asleep. Cory called her name, and she did not answer. China waited for Cory to fall asleep, and the tears ran down her face. China didn't sleep at all. She was able to shut her eyes at dawn into a depressed sleep.

China woke up the next morning extremely sore. Cory gently massaging her back asked, "Good morning dear, are you going to stay in bed all day? Shake a tale feather."

"Honey, I think I'm going to work from home this morning. I am exhausted from last night. It must have been those late evening drinks," she responded. She laid in the bed without moving an inch.

"Okay. Do you need me to get you anything before I leave?"

"No thanks. But, if you could close the blinds a few more minutes that would help a great deal. I'll call you this afternoon. Love you."

Cory kissed her and he left the room.

China heard the door close, and she begin to cry. The pain rushing through her body, would not allow her to move one inch. She had to call her office to tell them that she would be out for the day.

"Good morning Charlotte," she greeted her office receptionist.

"Good morning Mrs. Jackson."

"Charlotte, could you please let Mr. Buckner know that I will be working out of the office today? Also, please don't forget, not to allow any showings at the Lent Estate until I could have a company over there to clean the floors. The long vacancy at the location caused dust to travel through the house. Please email me the cleaning service information so that I could send them there."

"Mrs. Jackson, you don't sound so well. I could call the cleaning service for you."

"No thanks, dear. I can do it. I want to be very specific with them on the areas that need the most attention."

"Yes, ma'am." Charlotte replied, and they ended the call.

China struggled to hang up the phone. She called the cleaning service, and asked them to meet her at the Lent Estate at twelve noon. China crawled her way to the bathroom, and ran a hot bubble bath. She soaked. She cried.

China took two pain pills and stumbled to get dressed. She grabbed the duffle bag from yesterday, and put the clothes in the washer. She then went to the Lent Estate to recheck the location.

When she returned to the scene, China checked to make sure she had all of her and Dirty's belongings again. She then went to the upstairs areas to make sure she didn't leave any evidence or blood stains. As she was walking past the master bedroom, she saw a coverless bed. She remembered that she had put the comforter and rug in the care giver's garage. She had to remove those items, and at least replace the comforter. She went through the closets and was able to find an extra comforter. The original owner of the estate passed away, and the heir to the estate lived out of state. *There was a very good chance that the comforter would not be missed,* she thought.

China drove her car to the care giver's garage and put the bloody comforter and rug in her trunk. She went back to the house to wait for the cleaning company. The cleaning company arrived. She watched them as they cleaned the house completely. She requested them to extra clean the leaving room area. She called her office from her car phone to tell them that the house had been cleaned, and asked Charlotte to reopen the showings.

Charlotte advised China of pending requests for viewings for the property.

China drove to a dumpster in a nearby alley to discard the comforter and rug. She wanted to make sure that the van was still in the river. She drove to the lake and did not see any signs of the van. It had to have sunk to the bottom of the lake.

China drove home. She felt pain gushing through her body. She took another bubble bath. She just sat in the tub soaking in a state of shock. She wished she was dreaming. She pulled herself out of the tub, and put her pajamas on. She lay in the bed. She fell asleep and awoke to the house phone ringing.

"Hello," China answered.

"Hey sis. What you doing home?" Nubia asked.

"I had a late night, and decided to work from home today."

"I know. I called your office and the secretary told me you were working out of the office today. I'm calling to tell you that Amber is out of the hospital, and I want take her on a surprise sister weekend trip. What do you think about that idea?"

"I think that's a great idea. I just got back. I feel like I've already neglected Cory a great deal the last two months. Hey, how about yawl drive up here for the weekend?"

"Hey, that may work. Let me talk to your other sisters. I will call you back this evening."

"Nubia, Cory and I may be out this evening. Let me call you back tomorrow. Okay?"

"Sounds like a plan," Nubia replied, and they said their goodbyes.

China decided to call Cory so that he would not worry about her. "Hey Honey. How is your day going?" China asked.

"Busy. How are you feeling?" he asked.

"I'm much better. I was able to work from home a little bit. I am resting. It has to be all the traveling, and then that late night evening meeting. I'll be great by the morning, I'm sure." China responded trying to ensure Cory that she was well.

"That is great to hear, my love. What else is new?"

"Nubia called, she wanted to take Amber on a weekend getaway to celebrate her being released from the hospital. I told her I just got back to my man. I invited them down here for the weekend. I will find a suite for them to stay in, and will come home to you every night."

"That sounds better than you leaving me. When you leave, you don't like to come back. You and your sisters should stay at the house, and I'll stay with Gerry. It'll be good for brothers to spend time together also. I'll see you when I get home. Love you."

"Love you, too." China replied, and she hang up the phone. She pulled the covers over her face, and cried herself to sleep.

China was awakened by a kiss to the forehead. "Good morning Babe." Cory said softly.

"Awe. Cory, can you please call my office, and let them know that I will not be in today. I feel really bad." China whined.

"I checked your temp. while you were sleeping last night. I didn't want to wake you. You don't have a fever. Come on, tell the doc. what is bothering you so I can help you get better?"

"I think I'm just exhausted. I have been doing way too much lately. I just need to take a day or two to stay like this," she explained. "Nothing is bothering me. I just think I need rest. I think my body is tired."

"Okay, but if this last for more than two days, we will be going to the hospital to run test. Agree?"

"Agreed." China replied, and she forced herself to raise up to hug her husband.

"I am going to check to make sure we have enough sick food to get you through the next couple of days before I leave for work. Are you sure that you don't need me to stay and take of you?"

"Honey, I'll be fine I promise. I'm not trying to go to the doctor. Have a great day. I will call you this afternoon."

China felt extremely bad. Not only was she lying to her husband, she could not believe that she was not dreaming. She began thinking that if she had just gone to the police that she would not even have been in this mess. And she thought, *I should have told Nubia or somebody.* The tears started to roll down her face. She heard Cory's car pull out of the garage. Her body felt like she had just been hit by a truck (she imaged that's how it had to feel). She could not even roll out of the bed. She had to move around. She had to get better. If she was taken to the hospital, she thought they would find out about the struggle, and she would have to tell Cory what really happened.

China stood up out of the bed. She cried with every step. She ran herself a hot bath and soaked for an hour. She got up, put her pajamas on and waddled down the stairs. She turned the television on to make sure there wasn't any news about what had occurred. She checked her emails. There was a message from her boss Mr. Buckler wishing her well. She replied *"Thank you Sir. I'm just exhausted from doing a little too much. I should be back to work by Thursday, Kindly, China."*

China made herself a cup tea, and just sat on the sofa in a daze. The telephone rang. "Hello," China answered the phone.

"Hey baby sister. What is going on? Do I need to come, and lay hands on you?" Nubia asked.

"Very funny. No I think I was just a little exhausted that's all. I was just about to call you." China responded quickly, changing the subject. "Are yawl coming down this weekend?"

"Not this weekend. But, we can make it next weekend. How would that work for you?"

"That would be even better. Cory is having brother time also. He's going to Gerry's. So we'll have the house to ourselves. I can't wait. I will see yawl then," China replied, and she hang up the phone.

She confirmed the following week's plans with Cory, and she told him that she was feeling much better after drinking tea. He told her that their agreement was still standing until he felt she was 100%. They wished each other good afternoons and hang up the phone.

Chapter Thirteen

CHINA WAITED ANXIOUSLY AT HER front window for her sisters to arrive from their road trip. She was beginning to feel like herself again. Cory was at his brother's for the weekend. China was finally going to be able to host her sisters in the town, she called home. She had the whole weekend planned out. She was hoping, when they found out how great it was in Caryville that they would not want to go back to New Berry.

She heard a car pull into the driveway. She ran to the door, and saw a van pulling in. She ran to greet her sisters. They hugged as if they hadn't seen each other in years. China especially hugged Amber. Tears began to roll down their faces.

"Come on yawl, let's party." China said as she helped carry their bags into her home.

"Wow, this is nice." Donte said, looking at China's oversized home.

"Everyone, please make yourselves feel at home. There are only four guest bedrooms. *Somebody* gone have to share. But, two of the rooms have a bathroom. One of you who get the bathroom should probably share in all fairness. I will let yawl figure it out." China explained.

The sisters ran up the stairs to pick their rooms. Alexa and Amber shared a room. After they washed, they went to the dining room where China had prepared a Mexican Style dinner for them.

"I am sooo hungry," Tena said.

"So how was the drive down?" China asked as she ate a taco.

"It was drama filled. You know how your sisters could be." Tena added. "And those two argued about everything in sight," pointing to Donte and Amber.

"Well, I am so glad yawl are here. Amber I am so glad to see that you are doing better. You are too good to let life have you down," China said. She handed her sisters sheets of paper. "Here is the agenda. I have a party planned at this local club tonight for Amber. When we finish eating, we should get dressed."

"Wow, this is great." Nubia said as she skimmed the agenda. "But, I don't see church on the list for Sunday Morning. Now you know that I cannot miss giving God, His time."

The other sisters were not into God, as Nubia. They believed in God. But, every Sunday worship was not a practice in their lives.

"We can definitely attend Caryville Baptist. That is where I go, when I can. Service starts at 9:00 a.m." China advised, and she updated her copy of the agenda.

"Awesome," Nubia said. "But, after lunch Sunday, we are going to have to leave because, Donte has to get back to the kids, before Andrew jumps out the window. He called her twenty-five times while we were in the car already." Everyone laughed, except Donte.

"I can't help it yawl don't have nobody that calls to check on yawl, like my man." Donte sounded in defense.

"Girl, checking on and nerve wrecking are two different things. Aint nobody mad at yawl though. Do yo' thang chicken wang," Nubia replied. They all laughed again. Donte could not help but to join in the laughter that time.

The sisters enjoyed each other's company the whole weekend. They celebrated each other and relaxed. They all told China the best time was the afternoon at the spa. They had first class treatment. Sunday afternoon, they wanted to extend but, knew they had to get back to their lives.

As they were walking to the van to leave, Amber pulled China aside, "China, does your offer still stand about me coming to stay with you for a little while?"

"Always. Just say the words. You don't even have to ask. I could ask Cory to get you a job at the hospital." China replied without hesitation. "Would you like to stay here for another week to see how you like it?"

"I have to go back to outpatient therapy. But, I only have six weeks remaining to complete the session. Maybe after that. I will call you to let you know."

"I am here. And you are always welcome. Please don't ever forget it. Hang in there. Remember you are too good to be in bad places. I love you so much," China replied, and they hugged each other.

They all hugged their goodbyes. China and Cory wished them safe travels.

Cory gave China a hug and the biggest kiss. China knew that she could not keep rejecting Cory's passion, or he would begin to feel neglected. She had to return passion. She and Cory had not made love since her attack. She had to, or she would have to tell Cory what happened so he could understand. She thought that if she told Cory what happened that she would have to tell him everything. She was not ready for that.

They walked into their home. Cory turned on the slow jams, they danced. Cory held China so softly. He began to rub her body gently. China did not resist. They walked up to their bedroom and made love. China held back the tears. Cory fell asleep, holding China in his arms. The tears streamed down China face like a faucet.

"Good morning Charlotte." China said as she walked into her office.

"Good morning Mrs. Jackson. Here are your messages. Also, Mr. Buckner is calling a meeting with all associates and brokers at 10:30 in the large conference room. I have already rescheduled your showing for the Adams Estate at that time. It's now at one-thirty, this afternoon."

"Awesome. Thank you," she said, and she walked into her office.

Mr. Buckner walked into China's office. "Good morning China."

"Good morning Mr. Buckner."

"Escrow closed this morning on the Lent Estate."

"Amazing. That was quick," she said, enthusiastically.

"It was. I think it sold quickly due to your hard work, with marketing of the property. Her son has expressed his gratitude, and he has also referred your name to several of his lawyer associates in the area."

"That is so good to hear."

"Charlotte told me about the meeting this morning. Is there anything I need to prep for?"

"No, it's more of an announcement than a meeting. I'll see you then." Mr. Buckner replied.

China walked into the conference room at 10:15, sharp. She was the only one there for a few minutes. Everyone else walked in at the same time, with a lighted cake and balloons. China was overly surprised.

"What's all of this about?" She asked smiling.

"China, since you have been at this agency, our sales have soared greatly. I would be remissed is I do not step up and allow you an opportunity. At this time, I would like to offer you a partnership in Buckner Realty." Mr. Buckner said.

China was in awe. She had to say something, the whole office was standing there looking at her.

"Mr. Buckner, I would be honored. I didn't expect this. But, I would accept the offer tentatively until I have time to review the terms of the partnership." China replied.

"Of course you would. That is what makes you such a valuable asset to this company. I can have my lawyer present the offer to you in writing. There is no rush. Even if you do not accept partnership, you will always be more than welcomed to remain here as broker as long as you would like. I surely hope forever," he said smiling.

"Thank you sir. I will let you know for sure after I review the offer."

They had cake and champagne at 10:30 in the morning, in celebration. China couldn't help but feel so grateful. At the same time, she still could feel a cloud hanging over her head. She ran to her office to call Cory to share the great news with him.

"Hey honey, Guess what just happened." China replied.

"Uhm, you are downstairs waiting for me to come give you a kiss?" Cory asked.

"No, silly. Mr. Buckner just offered me a partnership with the company."

"Babe, that is amazing. Well, are you going to accept?"

"I have to review the terms of the offer with a lawyer, and I have to think about it. Partner is great. But, I'm not sure if I want to be a partner, or be owner of my own company. Let's talk about it this evening."

"We will, and don't plan to cook. I am taking my executive out. Be ready by 6:30 please."

"Okay. I love you."

"I love you too. Bye," Cory said, and he hung up the phone.

China finished her showings and went home to get dress for the evening. The phone rang. "Hello." China answered.

"Hey sis." It was Amber.

"Hey Amber. How are you doing?"

"I'm well. My therapist said that I'm doing so well, that I could finish my program earlier than the normal six weeks. I think I'm going to come down and hang out with you for a while. There is nothing here for me."

"Sure. Do you need me to send you a train ticket?" China offered, knowing her sister was not getting on a plane.

"No thanks, I got it," she replied. "I will be there next month. Are you sure it's okay with Cory."

"Why, he would be more than happy. I mentioned this to him when you guys left, and he said that we don't even have to ask. He also said that the hospital always has openings. When you come, we can work on putting a resume together for you. Also, there are groups that you can get into to help you stay on track."

"Okay. Take it easy on me sister. My therapist said that I shouldn't feel pressured. That's a way to trigger a relapse."

"Oh, I'm so sorry. I didn't mean to sound if I was pressuring you. I just think I'm so excited. Let me know the day that you have planned to book the train ticket so that I can take off work to get you settled."

"Oh you don't have to take off. I will come on a Saturday," she replied, calmly.

"Okay. Oh, I was just offered a partnership at my company. So, I may be able to offer you a position as my assistant, if we don't find anything at the hospi…" China caught herself. "I'm doing it again aren't I?"

"Girl, I understand. That's fine. We can talk about that when I get there."

China began to feel an uneasy feel in her stomach. She went to drink a teaspoon of pepto bismal.

Chapter Fourteen

"BARSTON REALTY, HOW MAY WE serve you today?" Amber said, as she answered the office phone.

China decided to start her own real estate company. She knew that if she took the partnership Mr. Buckner offered her, it would be close to permanent, and she did not want to limit success. She decided to name it after her maiden name, and in memory of her late mother. She thought that Jackson was too common a name.

China's business was only opened a few months, and she had already established clientele, and was bringing in a substantial amount of income.

Amber moved to Caryville four months ago. China helped her take a customer service class at the junior college, and she hired as her as her office assistant. China had trained her on writing contracts and offers. Amber was doing quite well office-wise. Reality wise, she was still a little absent minded.

"Amber, can you please pull the Randolph File. I have a buyer who would like to place an offer on their property?" China asked.

"Okay. Do you need me to draw up the offer?"

"Naw, I got it. Also, I have someone coming to interview at 12:30 for a sales person position. He just got his license, and seems pretty established in this area. Please clean up the conference room so that he will want to join our team."

"By team, you mean, you and me, right?" Amber asked, jokingly.

"Whatever ma'am." China replied, and she walked into her office. Their office was not as big as the Buckner Office, but, it wasn't bad to start.

"China, I forgot to tell you that I have started looking at apartments."

"That's great Amber. Are you sure you are ready. I mean you, can stay at our home as long as ever, you know that right?"

"Yes. Thank you. I feel like I am out growing the Jackson Mansion. I am ready to branch out."

"Now girl, you know that house is hardly a mansion. I took you on showings with me. Compared to those real mansions, you know that my house is not even close."

"I know. Just kidding. You know you are not supposed to be yelling at me. You know my therapist said that could trigger a relapse," Amber replied. China knew that she was serious.

China looked at Amber, and in her mind counted down from 10. Her sister relocating to Tennessee was the best thing for Amber. But, has been quite stressful for China. China had to count down daily to control her temper. Amber always referred to her therapist and relapse. China knew that she was still a little off. Every other day, Amber would say some type of reaction could trigger her relapse.

China began to feel happy that Amber thought she was ready to move out. China could begin to regain her own sanity.

"Sorry Amber. Let me know if you need me to help you find something. I mean it's what yo sister does?" China replied, and smiled.

"I got it. I learned a lot from you. I am even thinking about taking a real estate sales class myself."

"That would be great. Let me know what I could do to help." China said as she walked back into her office.

China and Amber was on the ride home from the office, and out of nowhere, Amber begins to talk about Ray Ray.

"So, when I was released from the hospital back home, I didn't even want to go to the clubs and places I used to go to anymore."

"That's great. That means that you have healed well."

"I was looking for Maura and Ray Ray so that I could tell them not to ever call me anymore."

China couldn't believe what was starting to happen again. "Why would you want to find them? Let bygones be bygones."

"My therapist said closure is a part of my healing process. I felt that if I rid them of my beings, that I would heal better. I couldn't find them anywhere in sight. I told Nubia that if she saw either of them again to get their number so I could call them."

"Well, even if they don't call, you should feel closure because you moved all the way here. That's a lot of progress."

"No, that is not the same thing. I have to tell them to stay away from me."

"Amber could I ask you something?"

"Yeah. What?"

"How did you even get involved with Ray Ray, and Dirty, and them in the first place?"

"One day, I was at the club and I was minding my own business. This was right around the time that you graduated college. Dirty came up to me and asked me my name?" she explain. "At first I was like, scoot now get a way. But then, he started to wear on me. He began to buy me drinks. One day I went to his house. That was the first time that I ever got high. Dirty introduced me to a whole new world. He would ask me questions about my family, and especially you."

"What questions did he ask you about me?"

"He would ask where you were. And were you married? And what type of work you did?" Amber continued. "I always wondered why he kept asking me questions about you. Then he started to make me resent you. He started to say that you were the reason that I was stuck in New Berry, still living with momma. I didn't know how he did it. But he really made sense to me." Amber went on, "my therapist helped me understand that all of that was lies. I don't believe anything Dirty said, anymore. When Maura got of jail, Dirty's behavior towards me changed. He started to demand that I plot with them to get money from you. He said you owed him money."

"Amber, I don't want to talk about this anymore. I will tell you this, and I don't want to hear anything about any of those people ever again. Dirty was a bad person. All of them were bad, except for Maura. I have never done anything to any of them. They wanted money from me for no reason. I was a kid when I first met them through Crawl, and they have been trying to come after me since momma's funeral for no reason at all. Let's leave them where they are, and forget they ever existed. Okay?" China pleaded.

"China what did you mean when you said Dirty *was* a bad person. And all of them *were* bad? I mean you talk as if they are dead, or something."

The car was completely silent. China looked at Amber, and she quickly justified her answer. "I am talking as if they never existed. I suggest you do the same. Now what do you want to grab for dinner. I don't feel like cooking today?" Trying to change the subject.

They both answer, "PIZZA!!" and laughed.

Chapter Fifteen

AFTER FOUR MONTHS OF SEARCHING for apartments, Amber finally found an apartment. China believed that the place was suitable for Amber, and it would help with her healing. However, her health condition began to worsen. China reached out to Nubia to try to help her in getting Amber additional help.

"Hey sis." China said as Nubia answered the phone.

"Hi China. How are you guys doing?"

"Not so well. I think Amber needs more help. Every day she says things about her therapy. She rambles on about things that happened in New Berry. I think something happened to her tragically, and it is causing these episodes. One minute, she is fine. The next minute she is talking about I'm yelling at her, and her THERAPIST said that it will make her have a relapse. Help me please!" China pleaded.

"Calm down, Charlie Brown. Where is she now?"

"She felt like she was ready to move into her own apartment. That's where she is now?"

"Are you sure that she will be okay on her own?"

"I hope so. Do you have time to come down and stay with her a few days to check her out? If I ask to stay with her, she's going to say something about her therapist, saying she is going to relapse, and I am going to scream."

"Okay. I'll come down this weekend," Nubia replied, and without hesitation.

"Thanks. This trip is on me. Allow me to book your plane ticket?"

"Okay ma'am. That would be great. Book it for Friday evening, and leaving Sunday after church. See you then. Thanks." They said their goodbyes.

China's phone rang thirty minutes later. "Hello." China answered. It was Amber.

"Lady, did you tell Nubia to come down here, and check on me?"

"Amber, what are you talking about?"

"She just called me, and asked me if she could come stay with me. You got that big house. Why caint mother hen come stay with you? Yawl always messing with me. My therapist said that people better not mess with me. I am telling you that this is not good. Yawl gone see what happens. Ooh, ooh, ooh! She better not step foot in my direction," Amber was going completely off.

"Amber, I am on my way to your house now, hold on a minute," China replied, and he hung up the phone. Before she left, she thought to call Nubia.

"Hello." Nubia answered the phone.

"Nubia, what on earth did you say to crazy Betty?"

"I asked her if I could come down and see her new place. She went off and asked why I got to stay with her, when you have a mansion. She told me that she did not have enough room for me. I see now, what you are saying. She needs more help. I am coming down today. You do not have to book my ticket. Alexa is going to drive down with me. See you then. Love you." They hung up their phones.

China drove to Amber's apartment. She felt her stomach in knots again. She rang the doorbell. Without asking who it was, she was buzzed in. China knocked on Amber's door. Amber opened the door.

"Hey sister. I wish I would have known you were coming, I would have cooked you something. Come on in." Amber replied.

China just stood there in disbelief. This was the same person that just yelled her off the phone. She slowly walked in the Amber's apartment. She was playing oldies and singing.

"Come on girl cut a rug." Amber said dancing around.

"Amber, can we turn the music off for a minute and talk for a minute?" China asked, nervously.

"Oh, okay. Goodness. What you want to talk about now?"

"I asked Nubia to come down a few days to check on you. You seem a little off these days. I don't want you to have a relapse of anything. She said that you sounded unwelcoming?"

"Here we go again. Everybody, stop the world. Let's help poor, little Amber. Well, Amber don't need no help. Amber is good, as good gets."

"Amber, why are you talking about yourself in third person?"

China looked around Amber's apartment to see if she could see any clues about what was going on. "I like what you are doing to the place. I was going to offer to help you. But, it looks like you got it all under control. Amber, why don't you come stay with me tonight. I think you moved out too soon."

"China, I'm fine. I am not moving back with you. Nubia is not staying with me. And I am fine, fine, fine!" she replied, and rolled her eyes at China.

"Okay, how about I stay here with you for the night. We could sit up and make a girl's night of it."

"AAAAH! Would you stop it already!!!! I hate to be rude, miss, but it's getting late, and I need my beauty rest." She walked to the door to open it signaling for China to leave.

China walked slowly to the door, and tried to hug Amber, but she pulled away. China left. She listened at the door, and she heard the music get turned back up, and Amber talking to herself.

The next morning, Nubia and Alexa arrived at China's house. They all went to Amber's apartment. They were buzzed into the building.

They knocked on the door afraid of what would happen. Amber was in the kitchen burning bacon.

"Hey sisters!! I knew yawl were coming. I'm making breakfast?" Amber said.

"Amber, what are you doing?" Nubia asked.

"Can you hear? You need to get your ears checked. I said, I'M COOKING YAWL BREAKFAST!" Amber put the wooden spoon down that she was trying to flip the bacon over in the pan with, and began to use her fingers in fake sign language.

"Okay Amber, we have contacted your doctor in Illinois, and she referred us to another clinic here. We are taking you there now to get you help." China said.

"Yawl should have told her that it's all fault that I am this way. She told me that this would trigger my relapse. Yawl coming up into my secure home, and coming after me," she started to cry.

"Amber, no one is coming after you. You just need treatment, maybe some medication," China replied.

Nubia walked around to the stove, and cut the burner off. She pulled the bacon out of the pan with a fork.

Shockingly, Amber agreed to go with them to the clinic. The clinic diagnosed Amber as traumatically depressive, and said that she needed to be there for a few months to heal completely. The sisters signed her in. The insurance from China's real estate company paid for the treatment.

Chapter Sixteen

"GOOD MORNING LISA." CHINA SAID, as she walked into her office.

"Good morning Mrs. Jackson. Here are your messages. Also, Mr. Walters said that he will not be in the office until this afternoon. He will be at an open house, at the Brighton Property."

"Thanks Lisa." China replied as she walked into her office.

Lisa was hired as China's new office assistant after Amber left. Daniel Walters was a real estate agent that China hired to help out with her booming business. Amber had been in the hospital for three months now. She was scheduled for release in one month. China was hoping that she would want to move back to Illinois. China felt that Amber was too much for her to handle alone.

China sipped her morning coffee, and open the newspaper that lay on her office desk. The headlines read "*THREE BODIES FOUND IN A CREEK OUTSIDE OF CARYVILLE, TN.*" China could not believe what she was reading. She began to fill nervous in her stomach. She read the article. It said that a man jogging in the wooded area near the creek saw a glimmer coming from the creek, and called the authorities. The authorities pulled a van out of the creek. The bodies were not in the van. The bodies had floating outside of the van in the creek. The police are conducting an investigation to determine the identities of the bodies, and causes of death. The police said that they appear to be older bodies, one female and two male, all African American. They were able to pull the license plates from the van in hope to identify the bodies. They could not determine if the van belonged to either of the bodies pulled from the creek.

China began to cry. She did not know what she was going to do. She never thought to pull the license plate from the van. She began to hope that the van did not go back to Dirty, or any of them to determine their true identities. China began to worry. *Should she tell Nubia? Should she tell Cory? Should she hire a lawyer?* She thought, *there is no way that they would tie those bodies to me.* She would wait this thing out.

Weeks went by before China heard anything else. The hospital called, and said that they thought that Amber was progressing but, felt that she needed more clinicals prior to release. China agreed.

China arrived at her office one morning. She opened the morning paper. The headlines read: *"THREE BODIES IDENTIFIED."* China began to read. They identified Maura though her existing thumb print, and by her having a criminal record. Most of her fingers had deteriorated. They were able to identify the other bodies through relationship of Maura. They said Maura Michaels, Raymond Michaels and Ellis Austin were the names of the victims. They said that Maura and Ray Ray were shot to death, and Dirty died from a knife wound to the neck. They said that no murder weapons were found. They have leads from a vacant apartment that they shared in NEW BERRY, ILLINOIS. China was stunned. She did not even think to travel to their New Berry apartment to search for anything to tie them to her. She began to feel very worried. She drove home.

"Hey babe," Cory was waiting for her with drinks.

"Hey Honey. How was your day?"

"It was fine. How was your day?"

"Very busy."

"Busy is good, right?" Cory smiled. "So, did you read the paper this morning?"

"I haven't had a chance to yet." China lied.

"They identified three the bodies from the creek. They apparently are from your home town?"

"I wonder who they were." China replied trying to find out what else Cory knew about what happened.

"They were some people named Michaels. Sound familiar?"

"Not really. I need to see their pictures."

"They did not show their pictures yet. Who would have thought anything could happen like that in our community. This has everyone all freaked out. The police are saying that it's an isolated incident. They are trying to assure everyone that this was random and has nothing to do with anyone in our communities. They are going to break this case before the whole town leaves."

China began to feel extremely nervous. She could not show any signs, though.

The next morning, her doorbell rang. It was the police and the sheriffs. Cory answered the door.

"Good morning, sir. We are looking for China Jackson." China walked slowly down the stairs try to hear what they were saying.

The policeman noticed China standing on the stairs, "Mrs. Jackson, we have a few questions that we would like to ask you. Can you come with us?"

"Officer, can you ask her here? Does she have to go with you?" Cory asked.

"Sir, it would be best if she came with us." the officer replied.

"What is this about, do you have a warrant?" Cory replied.

"We don't have a warrant, but we can obtain one if that is what you would like." They noticed China appear at the door. "Mrs. Jackson?" The asked.

"Yes." China replied.

"Ma'am we would like to ask a few questions about the Michaels and Austin case. Would you mind coming with us please? There is no reason to be alarmed, it's just routine questioning."

"Sure," she replied and she walked out to with the police.

"China, don't say one word, I am calling a lawyer." Cory said, and he ran to the phone to call the attorney.

"Hi. I am here representing China Jackson. I would like to let her know that I am here for her, and I would like to be in the room with her right now." Attorney Miles Anderson said, pulling out his business card and handing it to the desk sergeant. He appeared at the Caryville Police Station with Cory.

The detective came out, and advised Attorney Anderson that attorneys are not allowed in routine questioning. If she is arrested, they would allow him to come in to talk to her. They will advise China that he was present.

The detective entered the interview room where China was sitting. "Mrs. Jackson do you know the individuals that were pulled from the creek last month?" The detective asked.

"I'm sure I do if they were from New Berry, Illinois. My home town is very small."

"Can you please tell us how you know them?"

"I grew up with Ray Ray, and Maura was his mother. I didn't really know much about other person, Austin."

"When was the last time you saw any of them."

"I believe it was in my home town over a year ago."

"Do you remember going to the Illinois State Prison to visit Maura."

"Yes. It was an unforgettable experience."

"Why did you go to visit her?"

"Ray Ray and I were childhood friends. He was at my mother's funeral and mentioned that his mother was in jail. I hadn't seen him since we were kids, and I felt bad for him. I told him I would go, and visit her because he asked me to."

China began to think, how stupid was she to go and visit Maura. She forgot all about it. She hoped her reasons for going to visit made sense.

"Did you know that they were in Tennessee?"

"No. I had not seen them since I was in New Berry, last year."

"Do you know any reason why anybody would want to kill them?"

"I have no clue." China continued, "I really don't have anything else to say. I am sorry that this happened. If you don't mind, I would like to leave so that I can let my husband know that I am okay."

The officer left out the room. He came back in and held the door open for her to leave. "Thank you for your time."

China left out of the interrogation room into her husband's arms. They drove home. "What was that all about sweetie?" Cory asked.

"I have no idea. They found out that I was originally from New Berry, and I guess they are questioning everybody here that are from that area," China replied.

"Well, did you know them?"

"Honey, everybody in New Berry knows everybody. I knew of them. But, I didn't know much about them at all."

"I'm glad that's all over. I wonder if they will question Amber in the hospital."

China began to feel extremely nervous. She only hoped that they wouldn't question Amber. Surely, if *Amber found out that those fools were dead, she would implicate China,* so China thought. She would tell them about the blackmail, and China would definitely be a suspect.

On the way back home they stopped and grabbed dinner. The phone was ringing when they opened the door.

"Hello." China quickly answered the phone.

"Hey Sis. What's going on?" It was Nubia.

"Nothing. How are you?"

"The police were just here looking for Amber. They told us that they found the bodies of three individuals that lived in New Berry. Girl, did you know that they found Maura, her son and her pimp in the lake by the city you live in?" Nubia explain, sounding upset and worried.

"Yes. They called me into the police station as well to ask me routine questions about them. What were they doing looking for Amber?"

"They said that Amber new Dirty. They believed that he was her pimp. They wanted to know if she had anything to do with their murders. I am so worried. I think we need to call her a lawyer." Nubia began to cry.

"Nubia, calm down. Don't cry. There is no way that Amber's doctors are going to allow her to be questioned in her frame of mind. I'm sure she had hardly, anything to do with those people when they got killed. She has only been here a few months anyway."

"Well, this is all too strange. What on earth were they doing in Tennessee anyway?" Nubia cried more.

"Nubia, don't cry. Everything will be fine. I'm going to go to the hospital tomorrow to check on the Amber. I'll ask her doctors not to allow anyone to talk to her without her lawyer. I'm sure that she had nothing to do with any of this. The police just want to question everybody that knew them. What else happened while they were there?" China asked in suspension.

"They just asked questions about Amber and Dirty. They asked if Amber was happy when Maura got out of jail. They asked when the last time any of us saw any of them."

"Don't worry. Get some rest. I will call you tomorrow."

"Let me know if I need to come down there."

"Okay. Bye. I love you." China replied.

China began to feel a sense of relief. The gears were changing from her to Amber. She was not happy that Amber was in the middle. But, it sure is taking weights off of her shoulders. She thought surely if she could keep Amber quiet about the blackmail that she would be in the clear. Even if Amber mentioned the blackmail, the frame of mind she is in, the police would not take any of her testimonies seriously.

The next morning, China went to her office, and complete her scheduled appointments so that she could be clear to look into the Amber situation more. It was Saturday, and it was not much to do.

Chapter Seventeen

"HI AMBER. HOW ARE YOU feeling, sister?" China asked her sister, as she walked into the visitation lounge at in the psychiatric ward of the hospital.

"Hey China. I'll be glad when I can get out of this institution. I told the doctor that I was feeling fine. He said that he thinks that I need more counseling. There appears to be something that I am blocking from my child hood that he thinks we need to reach, before I can been healed. I think they are just keeping me here so that they can get more money. I am telling you girl, I am fine." She replied. Amber was in sweats. She looked like she was healthy.

"Well, you look well. I will talk to the doctor when I leave to see if we can get you out of here. Do you have any thoughts of going back to New Berry, or do you think you want to stay in Caryville?"

"I'm not going back to Satan Berry. That town has so many bad memories for me."

"Amber, do you want to talk about the bad memories?" China asked softly, trying to keep Amber calm.

"Now you sound like them," she said, pointing to the walls. "They keep asking me, *do you want to talk about this, tell me about that.* Don't they realize that if I could tell them things I would? I want to be better, too. I feel fine. It's just when people start pointing fingers at me, it bothers me. It makes me feel like I did something wrong."

"I want you out of here, too. That's why I am try to help. I'm sure the doctors here want the same. Well, if there is anything that I can do to help, please let me know."

"Help? Please. From day one, you and yo' sisters have done nothing but hurt. Yawl the reason I'm up in this place. I was perfectly fine til yawl had to put yawl five senses in my business. You know what? I'm not going back to New Berry, and I'm not staying here with you. Ima find my own spot. Yawl can just forget about me. I think that if yawl leave me be, I will be just fine." Amber cried.

"Amber, you know we are not going to forget about you. We love you. We want to help you. I think I am going to just go. I will come back next week, okay?"

"I may be up out of here by next week." Amber said, whimpering, and wiping her eyes.

As China walked out of the visitation lounge, she stopped by the nurse's desk to ask if she could see the doctor.

"Good morning Dr. Rodriguez." China greeted Amber's Doctor."

"Mrs. Jackson, good morning." Dr. Rodriguez replied, and extended his hand to shake hers.

"Can you please provide a status of Amber Barston?"

"Yes. She is coming along. But, she still needs more help. She has a huge wall up, blocking something from her past. And until we find out what it is, she will not get well. I don't think she'll hurt anyone. But, if we don't address the issue and get to the bottom of it, who knows what would happen. I will definitely keep you posted."

"Doctor, do you allow visitors other than family members listed on the call sheet to visit patients?"

"That's against policy. However, if visitors were to come and they are not listed, we would call the point of contact to authorize the visit. The only other exception to the rule would be government, or law enforcement personnel who have court orders to see patients."

"Okay. Thanks so much. And please keep me informed of Amber's progress."

"Will do. Have a great day." He replied, and China left the hospital.

On her way home, China began to feel nervous. She only knew that nothing good could come out of this whole mess. She had to find a lawyer. She had to come clean. If only that tape recorder had continued to record, she would have enough evidence to clear her name. There was nothing else she could do but, wait this whole thing out.

She called Nubia to let her know that she had visited Amber, and to see if there was any news on her end.

"Hey sister." Nubia answered.

"Hi Nubia. I visited Amber."

"How is she doing?"

"She is coming along. The doctor seems to think there is something she is blocking out to make her have these episodes. He'll keep us posted. I've tried to ask her if she wanted to talk about things, and she began to get upset. I left it alone. It's best that we leave her breakthrough up to the professionals."

"Wow. I will keep praying for her, and all of us. The police came back again. I told them where Amber was, and they are probably going to try and contact her. I also gave them your information for a local contact."

China thought to herself, *now why did she have to go and do that. She was in enough water in the mess already. Oh well. What was she to do?*

"Okay. I have to go back to the office. I will talk to you later this week. Love you bye."

"Love you too. Bye." Nubia replied, and they hung up their phones.

China walked into her office, and picked up the newspaper from her reception counter. Every day the newspaper published some type of update for the ongoing murder investigation. The people of Caryville were not going let the crime go without it being solved.

The updates read that they were unable to locate any of the murder weapons or any other leads as to why the murders occurred. They found out that the victims were checked into a local hotel, and that they were from a town in Illinois. They did not have any clues to why they were in Caryville or Tennessee. They have followed every lead possible. They assured the town that they will find the murderers. They will not leave any stones unturned.

China felt a sense of relief. She thought to herself that she did good by tossing the knife and gun. Her office phone rang.

"Barston Realty, how may we service you today?" China answered the phone because Lisa had already gone home for the day.

"Hey babe. I thought I would find you there." Cory responded.

"Hi honey. You know me well, don't you?"

"You know that's right. So, I was thinking that we could catch a movie tonight?"

"That would be lovely. I am almost done here. I have to fax an offer to another agent, and I will be heading home. I will see you in a few," she said, and they said their good byes, and hung up the phone.

China was about to walk out her office when she noticed a detective car parked outside. She eased away from the window. The detective was just sitting in his car looking at her window. China got the nervous feeling in her stomach. She turned off all the lights, set the alarm and walked to her car. She looked directly at the detective.

"Good afternoon Mrs. Jackson," the detective said.

"Hello Officer. Were you coming to see me?"

"Well, if you don't mind. I had a few more questions to ask you about the individuals that were murdered."

"I have a few minutes. Did you want to come in?"

"Oh, that won't be necessary. My colleagues in your home town of," the officer paused and glanced down at a note pad he was holding "New Berry, Illinois, searched the Michael's apartment and discovered notes and articles with your name and places of business on them. We were wondering if they ever tried to contact you here or at the Buckner Agency."

"Not that I am aware of. They may have, but, the assistants often took messages, and sometimes the clients would say they would call back. However, socially they never spoke with me at either location."

"How about your sister, Amber?"

"Amber? I don't believe so. Amber is in the hospital, or I would ask her for you. I just left from visiting her."

"Yes, she is in the Caryville Edge. How is she coming along?"

"She is making progress. When I go back to see her I could ask her if she had spoken with them." China suggested, trying to be helpful.

"That won't be necessary. We plan on speaking with her soon." The officer handed China a card. "If you could think of anything else, please don't hesitate to call me." The officer got back into his vehicle and drove away.

China thought, *this is not good. There is nothing I could do. Whatever happens, happens.*

Chapter Eighteen

"GOOD MORNING MRS. JACKSON." DR. Rodriguez said as China answered her cellular phone.

"Good morning Dr. Rodriguez. How is everything going?" China replied.

"I'm just calling you to advise you that there were police detectives here this morning asking Amber questions. She began to get upset so we had to end the questions."

"Thank you for calling me. I will be right over."

"Mrs. Jackson, that won't be necessary. We can't allow other visitors when one of our patients get that upset. That could worsen their conditions," the doctor advised.

"Give it a couple of days, and I will advise the nurses to expect you."

"Thank you. Also, please call me if I could be of any assistance," she said, and she hung up the phone.

China began to wonder what the detectives asked Amber, and what could have made her so upset. After a few days passed China went to visit Amber.

"Hey sister. How are we feeling today?" China asked Amber and she hugged her gently.

"What do you mean we? When you say we, if you mean me, then I am fine. I cannot speak for the rest of us."

"I meant it as you and I. How are you feeling, Amber?"

"I told you I am fine. I just wish everybody would leave me alone."

"Who is bothering you, girl?"

"You, the police, the doctors, the nurses, and everybody else in the world."

"Well, I don't mean to bother you. And I am sure that the nurses, and doctors are here to help you." China explained. "What did the police say to you that bothered you?"

"You know exactly what they said." Amber continued. "They come up in here asking me if I knew anything about Maura and Dirty, and how they were murdered. I had no idea. But, somebody in this room may know."

"Yeah. They found their bodies, along with Ray Ray's body in the creek outside of the town I live in."

"I wonder what could have happened to those *nice* people." Amber replied, looking at China out the corner of her eyes.

"Things happen. Neither you or I had anything to do with it, right?" China said, as if she was trying to coach Amber on what to say if she was asked about it.

"Well I don't know about you. But, I sure aint had nothin to do with it. I caint figure out what in the world they doing way down here in the first place."

"What else did the police ask you that got you so upset?"

"They asked me if I used to turn tricks for Dirty. They think I was upset when Maura got out of prison. They got me all wrong. I was relieved when that lady came back. She finally got that fool away from me. He was bad China, very bad."

"I know sister. You don't have to answer any questions you don't want to, and if you feel like you need a lawyer, don't say anything else to the police. They will try to use it against ...." China tried to finish, but before she could Amber interrupted.

"Girl, what do you me against me. I aint did nothing. In fact when the police said they were killed, I was up in Illinois in the hospital. So, they definitely aint got nothing against me. But, you on the other hand, where was China when all this went down? Uh-Huh. She was right here in the middle of it all. Somebody looking worried now."

"Amber, I didn't have anything to do with it either. I didn't even know they were here. But, like you said, you were in the hospital, and I'm sure whenever this happened I was doing things as well. I just want to make sure that you know that I am here if you need me."

"I wonder what the police would think if I told them about Dirty, and them blackmailing you. That sounds like motive to me. I think I may say in Tentiseee after all. Make sure you have some place really nice set up for me. I really would hate to say something that could tare down your little empire you built."

"You are kidding me right? You know I didn't have anything to do with those people. You know they were blackmailing me for no reason at all. I think the police would believe a sane, upstanding citizen of Tennessee than a nut job like yourself. Don't get it twisted sista, I aint some scared kid. Don't try me. When and if you get out of here, you will have nothing from me. I have done nothing but try to help you. I love you no matter what happens. Take care sista. Just for the record, I was always willing to help you, and be there for you. But, since you are trying to pull this useless crap, I will not help you." China said, and she walked out the hospital.

While China was driving home she began to cry. She cried so hard, she had to pull the car over. She started to think, *she had to come up with a plan. Surely, here sister would not be fit to stand trial. If the police question her again, she would just put if off on Amber. Amber would not go to jail, she would just remain in the hospital a few more years. If China took the fall, surely they would blame her for the other two murders and she only killed Dirty out of self-defense.*

Chapter Nineteen

CHINA WATCHED THE CHANNEL 7 News as she awaited the Caryville Sherriff's statement regarding the murder investigation. The residents were on edge the entire five months as the police conducted their investigation. China was relieved. The Sheriff announced that they are closing the investigation. They mentioned the only potential suspect was diagnosed by a highly qualified psychiatrist as not being able to stand a trial. They believed that she killed the victims due to some type of lover's quarrel. They assured the Caryville Residents that this was an isolated incident, and that neither the victims nor the suspect were from Tennessee. The crimes although sad were due to harm that one of the victims Ellis Austin caused on the suspect. He said that she was in a local mental facility being treated. When she is released she will not be charged because they had reason to believe that the crimes were some sort of self-defense; the prosecutor does not have enough to charge the suspect, there was no murder weapon, and no other evidence to pursue prosecution.

"Do you believe this?" Cory asked China.

"I really don't. My sister could not have done that to those people. Why would she. I am just glad all of this is over, and we can finally get on with our lives."

"So, what is the plan for Amber when she is released?"

"I'm not sure. I don't think she would want to stay here with this hanging over her shoulders. I am going to Illinois next week to speak with my sisters about it. We have to figure out something. I just don't want her released without having recovered fully. Oh, don't forget that we have that dinner with the Smiths. They have been asking us for weeks, and I have been putting it off because I wasn't sure I would be much company. Try to be ready by seven honey, please," she kissed Cory softly on his lips.

"Whatever you say, sweetness." Cory smiled.

They kissed good byes, and left for their offices.

China's cell phone rang on her way to work.

"China Jackson, may I help you?"

"Mrs. Jackson, this is Dr. Rodriguez. Do you have a few moments to come by today so that we can talk about your sister's condition?" he asked.

"Definitely. Would 10:00 a.m. be a good time for you?"

"Yes. I will see you then," he replied, and they hung up their phones.

China went to her showings, and advised Lisa that she would be back later in the afternoon. She asked her to call her cell phone for urgent matters.

China had no idea why the doctor wanted to see her so urgently. She just hoped her sister was okay. She hoped that she could finally get her life back in place. She has always been a law abiding citizen. She thought to herself that she did the world a favor by ridding it of Dirty. She felt bad for Maura. But, Dirty deserved what he got, even if she had to do it in self-defense.

"China Jackson, here to see Dr. Rodriguez." China said to the receptionist at the hospital.

Dr. Rodriguez came to escort China to the conference room. "Thank you for coming, Mrs. Jackson. We have made a huge breakthrough with your sister. We can't go into to many details. However, it appears that your sister was raped when she was twenty-three years old by your mother's boyfriend. She said that she didn't tell your mother because she didn't want to ruin your mother relationship, and she was scared. This is huge. Now that we found a source of what could be the root of her sickness, we can work on the treatment plan. We have a clinic that we would like to move her to in Connecticut. They are the best for this type of treatment. If everything goes as planned we could have her in civilization in six months to a year. We could treat her here, but, I highly recommend the Connecticut Center."

"Dr. Rodriguez, this is all so much. I am in shock. I had no idea. I meet with my other sisters next week. We will need to decide as a group on treatment. Is there an equal facility closer to Illinois, in which Amber could be treated?"

"There are facilities in Chicago. They have some of the best hospitals there for your sister's condition as well. Allow me to talk with the center in Connecticut, and see if they could recommend a location. I'll get back with you by the end of the week before you meet with your sisters. Thanks again for coming." Dr. Rodriguez said, and he walked out the room.

China wanted to talk to Amber at least to give her a hug. She and her sisters had no idea that Amber had been raped by Willie, their mother's boyfriend. She wondered if anyone else in the family knew about it.

Amber walked in the room. "Hey China. I'm glad you could stop by. I see you in the clear. They let us watch the TV's here if we act like we got sense."

China walked to Amber to give her a hug. Amber stood with her hands to her side.

"Amber, the doctor said that you guys have made progress, and you are really close to coming home."

"It's about time. I will never come back to one of these places again. I don't care what you and yo' sisters do. This is the last time. They better heal me completely because this is it. So, when did they say I will be able to go home?"

"They said six months to a year. They want to move you to this special facility that can help you with a speedy recovery."

"What special facility, it better not be a place where psychos are. I mean, I have fits every now and then, but I aint nowhere near crazy."

"It will be either Connecticut or Illinois. We want to get you the best help so that you don't every have to come back in one of these places again. I go to New Berry next week to talk to the other sisters. Please let me know your thoughts so that I can tell them. We are all so concerned about you. We can't wait for you to come back." China said, trying to sound reassuring.

"I hate New Berry. I hate Illinois. I hate any city that start with N and any state that start with I. I aint goin back there. So, it would have to be Connecticut. And why caint I stay up in here to get it over with?" she said, and sounding like she really wanted to help.

"If you stay here, it would take longer to treat because their doctors are not as specialized in your condition as the doctors in the other states. It can be the Connecticut Facility. It's just that you don't have family there. Someone needs to be by you so that we can visit you. I'll see if we can take turns flying in. But, don't worry about it sister. You are going to be okay, and we will be waiting for you. Hey, when you come home, we can go on a sister girl vacation. You can pick the spot. I have to go because, I have so much to catch up on. Love you." She gave Amber a hug and kiss.

"I love you too. Tell everyone I said hey."

China went to clear up her emails at the office, and headed home to get ready for the dinner with Smiths.

Chapter Twenty

"CONGRATULATION BABE ON YOUR AWARD of being named one of Caryville's Top Real Estate Companies." Cory said as he and China sat eating breakfast at their newly built mansion.

"Thank you honey. I couldn't have accomplished this success without your support."

"So sweetheart, now that we both have reached our career success goals, do you think we can start our family so that our legacy can remain on earth long after we depart?"

"Depart? Where are we going? We are living forever," she replied, and they both laughed. "Darling, I would love to start our family. Let's get to it." She said as she walked to the other end of the dining table to kiss her husband.

"Let's start tonight. I have a patient to check on for release. I don't want to start nothing I can't finish."

"Okay. I have a meeting in thirty minutes anyway. I'll see you tonight." She said, and they both gathered their briefcases to leave for their offices.

China had established a top rated real estate company over a short period of time. Cory continued on at the Vanderbilt Hospital as a highly skilled heart surgeon. China was in her early thirties and Cory was in his mid-thirties, and they were doing quite well.

"Good morning Mrs. Jackson. Here are your messages." Her new assistant, Brenda handed her the messages. Her last assistant Lisa, recently was promoted to real estate agent in the company. China now has five realtors and one broker besides herself at her business.

"Thank you Brenda. Is my 10 o'clock here?"

"Not yet. Would you like me to call them to confirm?"

"That won't be necessary. I'll be in my office. Please call me when they arrive."

Each morning China arrived to her office, she walked around, and greeted all of her agents that were present. She believed that her continued openness with her staff motivated them to want to come to work and do better. After her rounds, she went in her office to start her day.

The intercom sounded. "Mrs. Jackson, Mr. Riley and Mrs. Riley are in the conference room." Brenda announced.

"Mr. and Mrs. Riley." China greeted as she walked into the conference room. Mr. Riley was a profound professor at Vanderbilt University, and Mrs. Riley was a certified nurse who recently moved to the area and they was interested in purchasing a commercial property to start a daycare in the area.

"Good morning Mrs. Jackson. What do you have for us? We are so excited," Mrs. Riley said.

"I'm excited for you as well. There are a few locations I would like us to look at." China handed the Rileys the properties specifications. After they reviewed them, they advised China the locations they were interested in seeing.

"Shall we?" China said, and she motioned for them to leave for the showing.

On their way out, Brenda asked for a moment. She whispered, "Mrs.

Jackson, your sister Amber called. She said that you can reach her at this number." Brenda handed China the message slip. China stood in shock for a brief moment, and took the slip, and thanked Brenda.

After the property viewings, China hurried to her office to return Amber's call. "Hello." Amber answered her phone.

"Amber? Hi, this is China."

"Hi sister. How is everything going?"

"I'm fine. How are you? Are you still in the hospital?"

"Nope. I've been out of the hospital for about eight months now."

"That is great to hear. I wonder why I wasn't called when you were being released. All of us would have come to pick you up."

"That wasn't necessary. I'm completely sane now. I've been doing well."

"I'm so happy to hear that. You sound great. Where are you so that I can call the others so that we can come and get you?"

"Nope. That won't be necessary. Yawl will hear from me when I want to speak to yawl. I've already called the others. I will definitely see YOU soon. We have things to talk about."

"I can't wait. I have mo..." China tried to finish her sentence. Amber interrupted.

"Oh, Mrs. Jackson, there is no need for you to fill me in on updates. I know exactly what you are up to. I will talk to you soon. Bye." Amber hung up the phone.

China looked at the phone number that Amber called from. It wasn't a Caryville number. She couldn't figure out what area code Amber was calling from. She called Nubia to see if she knew anything about Amber.

"Hello." Nubia answered the phone.

"Hey Nubia," they greeted each other as usual.

"I just received a strange call from Amber. Has she called you, yet?"

"Yes, she called yesterday. She said that she was fine, and that she will call us when she wants to. I told her I love her and we said our good byes."

"She called me today. She does not want us to know where she is. I offered to help her, and to come and get her. I didn't know she has been out of the hospital for either months now. I'm beginning to worry about her. Where is she living, and where is she getting money?"

"China, don't worry about that lady. All we can do is pray for her. We have tried our best. She sounded okay on the phone. You have your own life to live. You have a great business, a great husband, keep living. Amber will be fine."

"I can't help it. I feel really bad for her. You know she had a hard life."

"I know. But, let her live on her own for a little. We need to start planning a sister get away. Those are so fun. We all need to relax. I'll call you next week after I talk to the others to see what they want to do."

"That sounds great. We need to do something soon. Cory and I have decided that we are ready to start having babies."

"I can't wait. Hurry up please." They laughed, and said their good byes.

China decided to listen to Nubia. She went home, and Cory was there waiting for her. He was sitting at the dinner table, with wine, and candles lit. They definitely started trying for their family that night.

Chapter Twenty-One

"CORY, C.J. LOOKS JUST LIKE you." Mrs. Jackson, Cory's mother said as they looked at the newborn through the baby suite at the hospital.

"I know mom. I can't believe how another life could come into this world so perfectly. I still don't get that, and I am a doctor." He smiled as she hugged his mother shoulders looking at his new son.

"I plan on staying with you guys as long as you want to help. I don't have anything else to do." Mrs. Jackson replied.

"Mom, you know that we already hired a live in baby sister from the church. But, you are more than welcome to stay. I know that you want to be with your new grandbaby."

"I will. I already put my things in one of the rooms." They laughed.

China walked into her home from the hospital, and Cory had surprised her. All of her sisters were waiting with a surprised baby shower. They knew that China would still be recovering, so it was just them. China cried. She looked over in the corner, and there was Amber. She was smiling, and were tears falling down her face.

"Oh my goodness. Amber?" China said as she walked slowly over to hug Amber.

"Hey China. I am so happy for you."

Everyone sat on the sofas looking at Cory Jr.

"He is so precious," Nubia said. "Now you know that it is going to be so hard for us to leave here?"

"I know. I don't want yawl to go. I miss yawl so much," China replied.

"China, would you like me to take CJ, and lay him down while you sit with your sisters?" Mrs. Jackson asked.

"That would be nice. Thanks ma," she replied.

"China, if you want, I can stay a little longer to help out." Amber said out of nowhere. China looked up at Amber. Her sister looked calm. But, she looked old. Her hair had started to gray.

"That sounds good. But, you know that Tena does not live far; and Cory's mom has already relocated here for a while. But, you are always, more than welcome to stay here with no strings attached."

"Okay."

"Amber, would you like to share with the family where you are living these days?" China asked, softly.

"Nope."

"You know that you we are here for you, if you need us, right?"

"I know. I know exactly where to find each of you, if I need yawl. I am doing well."

The sisters began to pack, to return to their lives. China discreetly, gave Amber an envelope. Amber opened the envelope, and it was a check and a note, "*Start over, start fresh, start you.*" Amber put the check in her purse, and hugged China.

Epilogue

CORY AND I REMAIN IN Caryville. We are raising our son with the same morals, and values as we were taught. Nubia lives in New Berry; she became pastor of her own church. Alexa continues to work at a New Berry Hospital as a nurse; she finally started dating. Donte and her family moved to the Barston house; she has her hands full. Tena decided to follow in my footsteps as a real estate agent; she moved to Caryville in her own home, and is working at China's company.

Amber remains to be stateless. She still has not told any of us where she lives. She shows up at all family gatherings. We have decided not to pressure her. We pretend that she is sane because, we don't want to push her away.

It would be quite interesting for Amber to tell her story.

CPSIA information can be obtained
at www.ICGtesting.com
Printed in the USA
FFOW03n0743211015
17893FF